UNFORGIVABLE

ALSO BY AMY REED

Beautiful

Clean

Crazy

Over You

Damaged

Invincible

UNFORGIVABLE

Amy Reed

KATHERINE TEGEN BOOKS
An Imprint of HarperCollins Publishers

Katherine Tegen Books is an imprint of HarperCollins Publishers.

Unforgivable
Copyright © 2016 by HarperCollins Publishers
All rights reserved. Printed in the United States of America. No part of this
book may be used or reproduced in any manner whatsoever without written
permission except in the case of brief quotations embodied in critical articles and
reviews. For information address HarperCollins Children's Books, a division of
HarperCollins Publishers, 195 Broadway, New York, NY 10007.
www.epicreads.com

ISBN 978-0-06-229960-4

Typography by Michelle Gengaro-Kokmen
16 17 18 19 20   CG/RRDH   10 9 8 7 6 5 4 3 2 1

First Edition

For Oakland

UNFORGIVABLE

you.

YOUR HAND, MY HAND. I MEMORIZE YOUR FINGERPRINTS. The universe is the space between our bodies.

No need for words. Our skin whispers its secret language. Our bodies nod yes. Over and over, the motion like breathing. Yes and yes and yes and yes.

Love is an understatement.

But that was before. When you were still golden. When you were still here.

We made the sun.

here.

I'M SORRY. MEET ME AT THE BEACH. I LOVE YOU.

That's what Evie's text says. It hasn't even been two hours since our fight, since I dropped her off at home and she was so drunk she could barely make it to the front door. She said she didn't need me. She said she didn't want my help. She said we were over.

I shouldn't go. I shouldn't keep letting her call the shots, shouldn't keep running after her, picking up the pieces as she falls apart. I can't just keep watching as she destroys herself. That's not what love is supposed to look like.

But something tells me to turn around. Maybe she's sobered up. Maybe something I said got through to her. Maybe she wants to let me help her.

My car bumps along the rocky road to our secret beach by the Bay Bridge. Traffic zooms by on the freeway to my left, hundreds of people rushing to San Francisco, completely unaware of this stretch of sandy shore and the beautiful girl stranded there, and me, the boy who loves her.

I never told Evie I had a history with our beach, that it belonged to someone else long before I shared it with her. I never told her what I was doing there that day I found her in the tunnel a month and a half ago. There were so many things I never told her, things I planned to tell her later, when we had only just started.

Before the beach was ours, it was my mother's, and she shared it with my brother and me. It was a place of kites and shell-finding expeditions. Then Mom gave it up, David and I inherited it, and it became a place for doing things we needed to hide.

And then, fast-forward ahead to that day—the end of one world and the beginning of another: David's ashes in a metal urn in my backpack, stolen that morning from where they had been sitting for nearly ten months on the mantel in the living room, a room where no one lived. Dad's urn selection, Dad's placement—a prison for David, in death as in life. So I had decided to liberate him.

The day had been gloomy and wet. I guess it was fitting. It would have felt weird saying good-bye to David in the sun. Better that my jeans were sticking to my legs and my feet were sloshing around in my boots, that the honks of semitrucks on the bridge kept interrupting my impromptu eulogy, that the air smelled like rotting seaweed and car exhaust. I pulled the container out of my backpack and used a rock to pry off the lid. When I finally managed to dump the ashes, half of them got stuck on a floating plastic bag that I had to poke with a stick until it would go under.

There was nothing poetic about it, nothing cathartic. Just a pile of ashes turning into fish food.

And then David was gone. Not really him, I know that. Just what was left of his body—the packaging, the wrapper. The real him had been gone for almost a year, or maybe even longer. The version of my brother that existed before he died was no one I recognized. But it was done. That was it. All that was left of him were the houseplants he gave me when he moved out a year before his death and the pack of cigarettes I found in his room behind his dresser, the only thing that remained of his stuff.

After the liberation of David's ashes, I walked slowly across the beach, letting myself get drenched. It's always struck me as ridiculous the way people fight the rain even after they're wet, as if they can undo what's already been done. I trudged back to the abandoned bus stop, back to the stairway down into the tunnel that runs under the freeway lanes and tollbooths of the San Francisco Bay Bridge.

I stood in the dry tunnel, in the place where the pale light still illuminated the gray walls, listening to the muted rain and traffic. The lights were all out for some reason and it was eerie, and I smiled for a moment, thinking David was responsible from beyond the dead. I lit one of his cigarettes and inhaled, imagined smoke from the same batch of cigarettes entering his lungs, one last thing for us to share. I don't even smoke cigarettes usually, but it seemed like it was something I had to do, like there was some meaning there—ashes, cigarettes, the fact that they both belonged to David. So I forced the smoke down into my lungs, the stale tobacco burning and crackling. His ashes were on their way out to sea, but that smoke would go inside me. Particles would stick in my lungs and stay in there forever.

I whispered, "Good-bye." I walked deeper into the tunnel. I turned on my flashlight. I wanted to feel something more than what I was feeling.

And that is when I saw Evie, standing in the almost darkness, completely still, the hood of her raincoat pulled tight, revealing the perfect circle of her face. Her eyes were closed, her face serene, and the stillness was shocking in that dark place, the fact of seeing her so unexpected, before she knew I was there, the intimacy of watching her when she believed she was alone. Even before I knew her, I could tell this was rare, that I had stumbled upon something extraordinary. I felt like a thief. I was seeing something I had no right to.

If I had walked away then, I could have probably forgotten her.

It was Evie who said, "Wait." It was Evie who asked me for my number. It was Evie who opened the door to everything.

Now, here I am chasing after her. It is me asking—begging— her to wait.

"Evie!" I call when I get out of the car. I don't see her. She's not walking on the sand, not sitting on a piece of driftwood. Maybe her text was a prank, one final way to hurt me. Maybe she brought me here to confirm she's gone. No. As low as she's gotten, I can't believe she would ever be that cruel.

But where is she? I look among logs of driftwood to see if maybe she's lying down between them, as we did when we camped here two nights ago, when our love still seemed salvageable. We broke through something that night, and even though Evie was drunk, I knew it was real. Her tears were real. The stuff she told me was real—her fear of letting people down, her self-doubt, her loss. She let me in, just a little, but the next morning, when she sobered up, she pushed me back out again.

And now there's a hole in me that's raw around the edges where she tore herself out. "Evie!" I yell again, into the sound of traffic, the sound of waves lapping against the shore.

The water. Evie loves to swim.

I turn around and my eyes focus immediately on a pile of clothes I had assumed were the usual beach garbage. But now I see a shirt I recognize. A pair of pants. My blood goes cold. My veins are slivers of ice inside me that go straight to my heart.

She was so drunk. The water is so cold.

I tell myself this is a dream. I will wake up any second and Evie will be next to me, and we will be lying in the grass and we will be part of the earth and there will be no water anywhere. I want to close my eyes and make this all go away, but they fight my fear and stay open, searching for her. I try to keep my focus on shore, but I keep looking out to where the water gets deeper, colder, darker.

"Evie!"

I hear my voice. It is far away. My body runs, but I do not feel it.

I see skin. A body, submerged. Unmoving. Wet hair, the back of a head. No face.

Evie told me once that swimming was one of the few things that made her feel free.

I am in the water, and all feeling comes back to me. I am in my body, suddenly and completely, stinging with cold. My clothes drag as I swim, but it would be too much trouble to take them off, even though I know this is how people drown.

I am halfway there. I am either halfway to saving Evie, or halfway to knowing it's too late.

When I finally have her in my arms, the first thing that crosses my mind is that this is the first time I've ever held her and haven't felt a fight.

Her eyes are closed. Her body's limp. I can't tell if she's breathing. I kick with every ounce of strength in my body to get her back to solid ground. One of my shoes slips off. The shore is forever away. I try to remember to breathe. I cannot swim and cry at the same time. I keep my head above water. I have to fight for both of us.

I pull her onto shore. All she has on is her bra and underwear, and even though we're the only ones here, my instinct is to protect her from eyes that have not earned the right to see her bare. She would not want to be exposed like this. She was someone who cared about privacy. She was someone who embarrassed easily.

Past tense? No. Not acceptable.

All I can think to do is shake her. I grab her shoulders and try to shake life, breath, sense into her. Her head rolls around and I feel guilty for shaking so hard. Maybe it wasn't necessary. Maybe somewhere deep down, I wanted to hurt her. Maybe she will break in my arms, her fragile bones shattering and all I'll be left with are sharp broken pieces, and they will cut into me like immovable splinters.

But then she coughs, deep wet and horrible, and relief spreads through me as the sea explodes from her body in waves. I hold her against me, my body an apology, and I give her all the warmth I have left. I can't tell who's shaking harder—me or her. She is alive, and that's all that matters.

"Evie," I say. "Can you hear me?" Nothing but choking, gasping, retching. The most beautiful sounds I have ever heard.

"Evie, wake up," I say, but she doesn't. And I know I can't wait for her.

I pick her up and cradle her too-light body in my arms as I run across the beach. She could weigh a thousand pounds and I would not feel it. Rocks and broken glass dig into my shoeless foot. But I run. It is the only thing I can do.

I pull out the blanket I always keep in the back of my car, the "emergency nap blanket" we always joked about. Until now, its purpose has been to hold us as we lay in each other's arms, to soften the world as we made love. And now I'm wrapping it around her freezing-cold body, begging her not to die.

I lay Evie down in the back of the wagon and drive like hell to Oakland Children's Hospital. If they saved her life once, they have to be able to do it again.

In the fifteen minutes it takes me to drive there, I am thrown between the terror of now and the sharp stabs of memory. My mind runs through a series of scenes in quick succession, like what I imagine happens when dying people see their lives flashing in front of their eyes. Except the life I see is that of Evie and my short but intense relationship, how it started with her shrouded in mystery and ended much the same. She revealed some things to me in small, precious packages—her surviving cancer, her friend who died, her alienation from a world of family and friends that could not see her as anything other than sick and fragile. I was able to pull these small pearls of truth out of her, but they add up to only a handful. The rest of her is still unknown, still locked inside somewhere deep and hidden.

Suddenly I am cold. I am shaking. Wet clothes hang off my body. I am sitting in a puddle. My bare foot throbs, and I don't know if the wet it feels is from the sea or if it's my own blood.

I feel Evie's body behind me, radiating pain and need and excruciating silence. I feel her drifting away. I squeeze my eyes tight as I speed through a red light, waiting for impact, waiting for some kind of proof of us, an explosion as big as Evie smashing into my life, as violent as the way love took me against my will and pushed us together, two people already charred, still smoldering embers, ready to ignite, waiting for each other so we could light up the sky.

And now this—drenched and heavy and crushed by gravity, back at this hospital where Evie received a death sentence before I even knew her. Barely two hours ago, this girl I now carry limp and blanket-wrapped in my arms broke up with me in a blind drunken rage. Now she's unconscious and nearly naked, and I'm dripping wet, limping, and missing a shoe. When we enter the hospital, the sight causes a commotion. Blood from my foot smears the floor.

Families take a break from their worrying to watch the people in brightly colored scrubs rush to pull Evie out of my arms.

The waiting room is too loud, too bright. A baby cries. A woman talks on her cell phone in a hostile, sharp language that cuts the air that is thick with the smell of burned coffee and disinfectant.

Someone's asking questions. Words come out of my mouth in explanation—vodka, floating, cold, unconscious. We move as we talk. They guide me through doors. Their hands are on her, poking, prodding, searching for signs of life.

I say her name: "Evie Whinsett."

"Evie Whinsett?" says a man behind me who is not a part of anything that's happening.

A doctor, frozen in space, eyes wide, stares at Evie where they've laid her on the gurney. Her bare foot hangs out of the blanket, so cold, so lonely. That breaks my heart—her tiny pink foot, exposed to everything.

A low, guttural sob bores through the core of me, so loud and deep it shakes the hospital. My body is an earthquake. My eyes pour rivers.

"Doctor?" says one of the nurses.

"I'll take over from here," he says, grabbing Evie's wrist. "Her pulse is weak. We need to get her on a monitor quick." I can barely hear him through my sobs.

"You're not taking her upstairs," says the nurse. "This girl is heading to trauma."

"I'm coming with you," he says.

"But you were just down here for a consult," she says, apparently confused. Then, with hostility, "This isn't your department, Dr. Jacobs. You can't just show up and steal our patients."

"She *is* my patient," he says. "I've been treating her for over a year."

"Jesus!" I shout, the hot rush of anger replacing my tears. "What is wrong with you people? Can you stop your fucking pissing contest and save my girlfriend?"

The Dr. Jacobs guy grabs my arm. "What is she on?"

"What? Nothing." I pull away, using all my self-control to not hurt him. But then I look at her, at her pale lips turning blue, and I realize I don't know. There's so much I don't know.

"At least I don't think so," I say. "But she was drunk. She was really drunk."

"Draw some blood for a tox screen," he commands the nurse. Then his demeanor changes; for a moment he is not a doctor. "Oh, sweetheart," he says to Evie quietly, privately, as if the rest of us are not here. "What happened to you?"

But the softness leaves as soon as it came. "You need to wait in the lobby," he barks at me. "We'll take it from here." Another nurse puts her hand on the small of my back and before I know what's happening, I'm walking away. They wheel Evie through doors that say AUTHORIZED PERSONNEL ONLY in big red letters, and even though all I want to do is follow her, all I want to do is cover up her foot that must be so cold, all I want to do is to hold her hand and never let go, I'm going in the opposite direction, and I don't know when or if I'm going to see Evie again, and there's nothing I can do. There's not a damn thing I can do.

And so I wait. Two hours. Three. My clothes begin to dry. My foot stops bleeding. A boy whimpers next to me as he leans into his mother. A girl across from me vomits into a trash can. My own lunch begins to unsettle, so I take a deep breath and focus on a nick in the linoleum floor—something safe and solid and not in pain. I imagine what it must have been like for Evie to spend a year of her life in and out of here when she had cancer, how it was only a couple of months ago that this stopped being her reality and I entered her world. How strange that I could love someone so much knowing so little about her past. How strange that it didn't feel strange at all.

I know who Evie's mother is as soon as she walks into the waiting room, even though I've never met her. Unlike everyone else who enters, her eyes don't search the room for clues of the next thing to do. She already knows where the front desk is. She is too comfortable here. She is petite like Evie, with similar features, a more subdued version of Evie's striking beauty. She looks kind. She looks like a good parent. But the fear in her eyes looks too much at home.

After checking in at the front desk, she sits on the other side of the waiting area, her face full of fear and love. She looks nothing like the evil, controlling monster Evie described. She looks like someone who has been put through hell.

I should introduce myself. I should tell her what happened. But I have a feeling she doesn't even know I exist. I have a feeling she doesn't want to know.

The doctor named Jacobs enters the room and Evie's mom immediately stands up. He hugs her and they talk in hushed tones so I can't hear what they're saying. It suddenly strikes me that I should leave. I should not be here.

I stand up and start toward the door, but it's too late. Dr. Jacobs points at me and I feel the air shift from sad to menacing. Evie's mom's eyes go wide.

I open my mouth, but nothing comes out. I turn my head to see how far away I am from the door, to see how fast I can escape.

When I turn around, Evie's mother is in front of me. Her eyes are crazed, murderous.

"You!" she shrieks. All eyes in the waiting room turn to us. "You're the one Evie's been sneaking around with? You did this?" Her fists pound against my chest, but I do not feel them. They are nothing against the sting of her words. Evie said the same thing just hours ago, when she drunkenly blamed me for starting her on this path of self-destruction.

"No," I say, because the other option is unthinkable—yes, I destroyed your daughter. Yes, I destroyed the person I love most in the world.

"My daughter's in a fucking coma because of you," she says with a final pound, then starts weeping.

"Coma?" I choke. Our eyes meet, and for a brief moment, all there is between us is shared pain, shared love, our shared hearts breaking. This woman hates me more than anyone else in the world right now, but for some reason I put my arms around her. I do it without thinking, and I'm not sure if it's more for her or for me, not sure which one of us is trembling more, if it is me or her holding the other up.

Then she pushes me away. Hard.

"Get away from me," she growls. Low. Guttural. The primal sound of a mother who may lose her child.

"I'm sorry," I say.

"Get out of here."

I step backward. She follows.

"Get out of here!"

She pushes me again. This woman can't be taller than five four, can't weigh more than 130 pounds. But right now, she could destroy me.

"It's time for you to leave," Dr. Jacobs says. "Now." His hand is tight on my arm, pulling me toward the exit.

"But Evie," I say. "I need to know she's okay."

"You should have thought of that before you got her into this mess," Evie's mom says, then crumbles into a chair, crying. Dr. Jacobs pulls much harder than necessary, and I feel something tug the wrong way in my shoulder. He waves a security guard over from the reception desk and Evie's mom sobs into her hands. The rest of the room watches the show, momentarily relieved of their own suffering. The sliding doors buzz open behind me and I give them what they want. I leave.

I leave without knowing if I'll ever see Evie again.

there.

THIS IS MY FIRST MEMORY: DAVID, MY BROTHER, SPINNING in our father's desk chair. The office is off-limits, of course. But David isn't afraid of Dad the way I am.

"Faster!" he yells as I spin him. "Faster!" I make my arms move at warp speed.

He could keep going forever, but my arms give out. I am only five; my arms are sticks. And he is eight, almost nine, and besides Dad, he is the biggest person I know.

When he gets off the chair, he stumbles around the room. He bumps into things. His laugh has something new in it.

"Your turn," he says.

"I don't want to."

"Trust me," he says. And I always do.

Books and drawers and file cabinets. These are the things at eye level. They blur into air as David tries to make me feel what he felt. The world is a tornado of chrome and dark wood.

"Stop!" I cry. I do not like the feeling of everything moving. I do not like the loss of ground.

"Wimp," David says.

I lie on the dark, soft rug. My hands dig in to make the world stop spinning.

"I'm dizzy," I say. "I feel weird."

"I know," David says, climbing back on the chair. "Isn't it great?" And he starts to spin again.

A beach, a blanket, my mother and brother. Three pairs of hands entwined. Three sets of arms and legs, one pink and two brown, sun warmed, salt kissed. Stomachs full of farmers' market strawberries.

Mom is in the middle, David and I on either side. Her hands are in our hair, petting us. She calls us her pups. The world is a swirl of blue and green and love.

Her hair is splayed out on the beach blanket, like liquid gold. I press my face into it, inhale the rainbow of her shampoo. I think, *This is what happiness smells like.*

This beach is our secret paradise, a place we discovered, our tiny desert island. We are the only people who exist.

I know the magnet inside David is stronger than the magnet inside me. I know it pulls Mom, just barely, toward him and away from me. I can tell she's holding David a little tighter. But I'm not worried. It's impossible to worry on a day like today, in a place like this. There's enough of her for both of us. We are infinite.

A pile of shells lies next to me, my great finds of the day. I will put them in my magic box back home where I store all my treasures, where I hide them away to keep them safe. David holds on to the line of a kite that floats high above us, halfway to clouds, halfway to heaven. I know he dreams of flying.

Across the sea is a giant city called San Francisco. We have no need for a place that big. Here, the world is the perfect size. We make it small and manageable. It is just big enough for us. We are just big enough for it.

"My boys," Mom coos. "My perfect loves."

The world is a painting on a grain of rice. We are small, microscopic. The whole world is here, our little kingdom. Mom is the queen, and she is a good queen. There is something good in the world, and it is us.

you.

WE WANTED TO PRETEND WE NEVER EXISTED. WE THOUGHT we could erase the past if our love was strong enough. We wanted to create a brand-new world that consisted only of now, only of us, a tiny island in space and time, with no room for our baggage.

But sometimes I feel like that's all we were—our baggage, our secrets, our fear, our shame. We always talked about wanting to live in the moment, but maybe sometimes "living in the moment" is an excuse for being in denial about everything else.

I'm sick of secrets. I'm sick of guessing what's going through your head. I'm sick of watching what I say to you, of always being afraid you'll get scared and pull away. I'm sick of settling for pieces of you, of only giving you pieces of me.

But now you're not here. Now there's something entirely new to be scared of.

here.

I COULDN'T SLEEP LAST NIGHT. EVERY TIME I CLOSED MY eyes, I kept imagining Evie with her eyes shut, her face ashen, tubes everywhere, machines pumping life into her body. I called Evie's cell, but it kept ringing and ringing. I called the hospital, but they wouldn't even confirm that she's a patient there. An hour later, I called again, hoping for a different answer.

As soon as the sky starts showing the first signs of morning, I get dressed and jump into my car, the neighborhood silent except for me and the birds, singing as if everything's still right in the world. The streets are nearly empty as I race the sunrise to the hospital.

"Can you tell me what floor Evie Whinsett is on?"

The receptionist looks at me like I'm crazy. "Are you family?" she says with her eyebrow raised, her lips strained into a thin line. She has already decided my answer.

I want to say yes. My heart says the answer is yes.

"If you come with a member of the family," she continues without waiting for me to speak, "they will be able to sign you in as a visitor." She says this without even looking at me, her gaze moved on to her computer screen.

"But I need to see her. You have to let me see her *now*."

"Young man," she says over her glasses. "I don't have to do anything."

"You don't understand." My voice is gruff, wretched.

"I suggest you discuss that with the patient's family."

"No!" bursts violently from my mouth. The air shivers and stills.

"I think you need to leave now," the receptionist says sternly, one hand moving from her keyboard to the phone. "Or do I need to call security to escort you out?"

Two days and already two threats of being thrown out by security.

I leave without saying anything. It is time to go to school, time to try to make it through the day as if my world is not ending.

I know this is crazy. I'm acting like a stalker. But desperate times call for desperate measures, and I'm desperate. I am the definition of desperate. You look up "desperate" in the dictionary and there's a picture of me looking like a stalker.

I only made it through half the day at school, and then left at lunch with the excuse that I wasn't feeling well, which isn't entirely untrue. I tried the hospital again, hoping for a different outcome, a different receptionist, but the same woman was sitting there. I turned around before she saw me.

Now I'm standing outside North Berkeley High, waiting for Evie's sister, Jenica. She doesn't know I'm here. I've never met her. All I know about Jenica is her name and the fact that she's a senior here and a good student. Evie told me so little about her family. The only reason I even know who I'm looking for is because I googled her name and found her Facebook profile. Total stalker move. But I had no choice. There are so few places where Evie's and my world meet.

The school bell rings its last note of the day, and for a brief few seconds there's silence. I hold my breath when the front doors burst open and students filter out, filling the air with their chatter. I wonder how my life would be different if I had gone somewhere like this for high school instead of Templeton Preparatory Academy. I look around, and the student body is like an advertisement for diversity compared to the mostly rich, white, all-male population of my school. Every ethnicity and culture and style and sexual orientation is represented here, and no one seems to notice. No one looks twice at me, except for a couple of girls who meet my eyes and smile shyly. It's the kind of place someone who never fits in could actually fit in. Maybe here I'd have found real friends. Maybe I wouldn't have spent the last four years feeling like such a misfit. Maybe I wouldn't have been so dependent on David.

Maybe if David had gone here instead of Templeton, everything would have turned out differently for him. Maybe he wouldn't have suffered the same overachiever burnout, wouldn't have felt the same pressure to be perfect and exemplary, wouldn't have been put on a pedestal in the same way by his classmates and teachers. Maybe he wouldn't have had access to the expensive drugs that destroyed him. Maybe he would have had a chance at something like a normal life, could have tried a more civilized version of "smart" and "popular." Or maybe trouble would have found him no matter where he went.

I scan the crowd for signs of Jenica and see no one I recognize. I wonder how many of these people know Evie, if any of them are her friends. It's strange to think that so many must have known her much longer than me. Some knew her as a little kid; they know her parents; they have a history with her beyond the last couple months. That's all it's been. A handful of weeks. That's all it took for me to fall in love so hard I can't think about anything else. A few weeks and I've turned into a crazy stalker.

Maybe one of these guys has kissed her. Maybe one of them was her first love. Maybe she loved one of them as much as she loves me.

The vague noise of voices suddenly condenses, a laser point of focus. *Evie.* I hear her name. I turn toward the sound and am surprised by the source—a small group of girls so unlike her, the sound of her name in their mouths makes no sense. Three cheer-leaders in full uniform walk by, huddled in the throes of gossip.

"Evie's still in the hospital," one of them says.

"I heard she OD'd," says another.

"I heard she drowned," says the first.

"I heard she tried to kill herself," says the third.

I consider following them, to see if I can glean any truth from their gossip, but then I see a face I almost recognize coming from the opposite direction. She walks closer, oblivious to my presence. She is so close I could reach out and touch her, but she has no idea I'm even here.

"Jenica," I say, and it comes out sounding too harsh, too hostile.

She jumps. Her eyes narrow as they size me up. Her features are sharper than Evie's, more stern and severe, but they are undoubtedly sisters.

"Jenica," I say again.

"Yeah?" she says with suspicion. "Who are you?" But before I have a chance to answer, her eyes widen and she seems to go through several emotions in a series of seconds. Shock, recognition, relief, sadness, and then burning, furious anger. "You're the Templeton guy Evie was seeing," she says, stepping toward me like she's ready to fight.

"Yes," I say, reaching out my hand to shake. "I'm Marcus Lyon. I'm Evie's boyfriend." The word sounds so strange in my mouth. I've been on plenty of dates with girls I've met at parties or shows; I've hooked up more times than I'd like to admit, but never anything serious. I've never been anyone's "boyfriend."

Jenica doesn't take my hand. Instead, she steps forward and pushes me in the chest, like her mother. "You asshole," she snaps.

I open my mouth, but I have no words.

"You fucking asshole." I think maybe she's going to hit me, but then the anger in her eyes loses strength, like a fire extinguished, and tears surface in its place. Without thinking, I put my hand on her shoulder, and she recoils from my touch. But as I'm about to pull my hand away, she leans into me, and I find myself holding her. Her arms are tight around me, her face buried in my sweatshirt.

After a few moments, she steps away, wipes the tears from her eyes, takes a deep breath, and stands up straight. "Sorry," she says.

"Don't be," I say. "Are you okay?"

"What do you think?"

I say nothing. I've never been good at responding to sarcasm.

"My parents think it's all your fault," she says. I open my mouth to protest, but she keeps talking. "They blame you for everything. They can't accept that Evie got herself into this shit on her own."

"Is she okay?"

"She'll be fine. You found her, right? In the water?"

I cringe at the memory. It is still so fresh. Evie is still there, lifeless, facedown in the water, every time I close my eyes.

"You got there just in time, apparently. Much longer without oxygen and she probably would have gotten brain damage. Not that her brain was working that well to begin with. What kind of idiot goes swimming in the bay?" Jenica looks at me, and her face softens. "My sister," she says gently to herself, and for a moment, I'm not even here. Then she takes a deep breath, stands taller, and is all sharp corners and steel again. "Sorry," she says, her voice strong and unfeeling. "I know I sound harsh. It's how I deal with things."

Evie didn't tell me much about her sister, except she's a bitch. But I don't think that's the whole story. People come up with all kinds of ways to pretend they're strong.

"I love my sister," she says, looking at the ground. "But I feel like I don't know her. I haven't for a long time." She looks up and her eyes are kind. Tired. "She's hurt us. My family. I don't know if we can fix what she's broken."

I nod.

"She hurt you, too," Jenica says.

"Yes."

"She hurt a lot of people."

"Tell me how she is. Please."

Jenica sighs. "She was in a coma," she says. "For, like, a day. Then she woke up. She's still in the hospital. They say she'll be there for a while longer." She shrugs. "No permanent damage. Evie gets off easy again."

"She's okay?"

"Yeah." She laughs coldly, all signs of her former softness suddenly gone. "Of course. She's totally okay."

"Will you tell her to call me?"

Jenica shrugs. "I might mention it."

"Can I give you my number? So you can call me and tell me how she's doing?"

She looks at me like I'm an idiot. "I'm not going to call you."

"Can I have your number?" My desperation level has reached

25

epic proportions. "I just want to know how she's doing." I am whining. I am begging.

"I have to go," Jenica says.

"Wait," I plead as she turns around. She walks away without responding and takes all my hope with her.

you.

I THINK I FELL IN LOVE WHEN I FIRST SAW YOU, BUT you were terrified. You were a small, wounded girl—alone, underground—and I was a dark figure emerging from the shadows. A black boy in a hoodie. A man in a place no one could hear you scream.

You pulled yourself into a ball, your eyes closed tight, and even then, before I knew you, my first instinct was to put my arms around you, to rock you until you stopped shaking. I kneeled next to you and babbled until you calmed down. Somehow I convinced you that you were safe, that I wouldn't hurt you, and the relief in your eyes when you finally looked at me took my breath away, like you had been waiting for me to find you.

In that moment, I knew our lives would be linked. I knew I had been waiting for you to find me, too.

there.

THE WALLS OF DAVID'S ROOM HAVE BEEN REPLACED WITH mountains, volcanoes. His windows are trees. His posters are vines. The toys on the floor are all kinds of killing things—vipers, tarantulas, carnivorous plants, Tasmanian devils.

"Hot lava!" nine-year-old David screams. I feel the heat in my feet as the carpet transforms. I leap to safety—the bed, a hovercraft.

David grabs my pajamas and pulls me to him, wraps his arms around me. "That was a close call," he says. "Too close."

He is wearing Mom's swimming goggles and a towel wrapped around his neck as a cape. For some reason we can't explain, this particular adventure is a pantsless one. His underwear are Batman and mine are Spider-Man. I am wearing my yellow rain boots. They are powerful boots, but they can protect me from the hot lava for only so long.

"The hovercraft is running out of fuel!" David exclaims.

"What are we going to do?" My heart is pounding hard in my chest. David is always the one with the answers.

He adjusts his goggles. "I think we can use the ship's borax capacitator to create the chemical reaction necessary to transform this planet's native plant life to fuel."

"Okay!"

"Here." He tosses me a pillow. "Use this hover board to keep you off the lava. Collect those specimens over there." He points to a pile of action figures in the corner.

I get to work. I pile the alien plants in my cape. "What's this?" I hold up a small creature, blue and fuzzy, with two arms and two legs, two round ears and tiny black eyes, a shiny black nose and a thin upturned mouth.

David gasps. "A baby," he says reverentially. "An abandoned baby."

"What should we do with it?"

"We have to take care of it, obviously." He jumps onto my hover board and gently removes the baby from my arms. We stand precariously on the tiny surface, a sea of lava boiling beneath us. David is so close I can smell the milk on his breath.

"We'll raise him as our own," David whispers as he rocks the baby in his arms. "He won't know he was ever alone." He kisses it on the forehead.

"I thought the creatures on this planet were our enemies," I say.

"Not the babies," he says, so seriously it almost scares me. "It's not their fault who their parents are."

It's one of those random Monday holidays when there's no school and the government is closed, so everyone is home when David's IQ test results come in. Now Dad, who never touches us, can't stop patting David on the back and putting his arm around him, calling him "my kid genius" with a goofy smile on his face. Mom keeps looking at him and getting all teary eyed. I can't tell how David feels about it. I can't tell if he's the same person he was yesterday.

We go upstairs to play Legos in David's room, which is where we usually play because that's where all the magic is. I'm working on a boat, but David's not building anything. He's rooting through the tub that must contain at least a million Legos, spilling them all over the floor. It's like he's trying to make a mess.

"Stop staring at me, Marcus."

"I'm not staring at you."

"Yes, you are."

"No, I'm not."

"Yes, you are!"

I add another piece to my boat. David removes a red piece from a blue piece and throws them across the room for no reason.

"I'm so bored," he says. Lately, nothing we do seems good enough for him. He's eleven, and I know this means he's almost a man.

"So you're, like, as smart as Einstein?" I say.

"Nobody's as smart as Einstein."

"But you're almost as smart as him?"

He shrugs. He's the only person in the family who doesn't seem to be excited about his new IQ.

"So you can do some stuff like him? Like come up with some really smart ideas or invent something really useful?"

"I guess that's what I'm supposed to do."

"What does it feel like to be so smart?" I ask him.

He shrugs again. David usually answers one question for every five that I ask him, so I figure he's not going to answer that one. I go back to building my boat. It is not an impressive boat, not something a genius would build.

"It feels like life could be really interesting," David says out of the blue, so long after I spoke that I have to think for a moment to remember what I even asked him. "Like there are all these possibilities, like maybe I'm really lucky or something."

He throws another Lego across the room. It hits the wall and thuds dully on the carpet. He kicks the tub; the millions of pieces inside shudder. "It's like I could do anything I want," he says. "But now everyone's decided it's their job to make sure I don't."

"Marcus, wake up!"

The world is shaking me by the shoulder. The world goes from black to bright. From sleep to terror.

It is David's voice. David's hand shaking me awake. He is the world.

"What's happening?" I mumble. I can't focus my eyes.

"Dude, you have to get up!" Whose voice is that? Not David's. Not Dad's. Jason? Is that David's friend, Jason? It must be. He's spending the night.

My eyes focus. Jason's face is too close to mine. I've never liked him. I like him even less now with him yelling in my face.

"David," I cry. "What's going on?"

"Get up," he says. "We have to go. Something happened to Mom."

The world shudders and comes fully into focus. Sharp. Bright. Images flash in my mind of Mom before I went to bed tonight, when she crashed into the kitchen, home early from some kind of event with Dad. She was wearing one of her weird dresses that has no arms and shows too much of her boobs. Her hair and makeup were all messed up and her feet were bare. Dad had to hold her because she could barely stand up.

"Go to bed," Dad told us before we had a chance to speak.

"What's wrong with Mom?" I said.

She would not look at me. She would not look at any of us. "I was doing my job, Bill," she mumbled to the floor. "I was charming, wasn't I? So fucking charming." Her face was painted with wet black streaks.

"Is she okay?" David asked.

"Is she drunk?" Jason asked.

"Just go to bed," Dad said. "Your mom is fine." He said "fine" as if it were a death sentence.

But she is not fine. She is in trouble. Something happened to Mom.

I jump up. I scramble to my dresser, pull out pants, underwear, shirt, socks. I pull off my pajamas.

"We have to go, dude," Jason says. "We have to go now."

"Hold on a second!" My heart is beating out of my chest. I'm going as fast as I can. I will never be fast enough.

"No time," David says. "Let's go." He pulls my hand, and without thinking, I go with him.

We are rushing through the dark, silent house. Down the stairs. Through the living room. I am scared, but David's hand is still around mine, so I know we are going the right way.

"Where's Dad?" I say.

David opens the front door. I step outside. The cool night air chills my skin. I am wearing only my Spider-Man underwear.

I look at David and Jason standing inside the doorway, the darkness of the sleeping house surrounding them. Something is wrong. They are inside and I am outside. They are dressed and I am nearly naked.

Smiles have crept onto their faces.

I open my mouth to speak, but nothing comes out.

"You idiot." Jason sneers. I try to find David's eyes for an explanation, but the door swings closed in front of me. I hear the door lock. I hear them laughing on the other side.

I cry forever. I cry all the tears I own. I am the most alone I have ever been. Everyone I love is behind that door, and I cannot reach them. And they do not care.

I wake to a blanket around my shoulders, David pulling me to my feet. "Come on," he says. "Get inside."

"Where's Jason?" I say.

"Sleeping."

"I hate him."

David says nothing, walks me inside, and closes the door behind us. I watch his back as I follow him up the stairs. It could be anyone's back, a stranger walking up the stairs, no sign of feeling, no remorse. No love.

I follow him to my room. He does not turn on the light as I make my way to the bed, as I lie down. I know I am too old to be tucked in, but right now it's what I want more than anything in the world. My arms and chest are lead as I pull the blankets around me and wait for David to speak. I look toward where I think he is. He is darkness against darkness.

"God, Marcus," he says. "Why do you have to believe everything I tell you?"

Nothing fills in the hole he leaves behind.

We are too little to be riding the BART train alone, but Mom can't pick us up for some reason we don't know, and Dad is in court and unreachable, so we are on our own. We are in our Carlisle Academy uniforms, the private K–8 all-boys school that grooms its students for Templeton Prep, where, according to Dad, we are both destined to go. David is a worldly seventh grader. He played spin the bottle at a party the weekend before where he kissed a girl in a closet and put his hand up her shirt. He has smoked a cigarette. He is an expert on all the things I want to know.

David holds my hand, and even though it makes me feel like a baby, I don't want him to let go. I wonder what he sees as he stares at the map. I wonder how he deciphers the list of fares, how he knows how much money to put in the machine to buy our tickets. He navigates us all the way through the downtown Oakland station, puts his arm out in front of me when the train approaches, to protect me from getting blown onto the tracks. It all seems like magic, and he is a wizard. I know without him, I'd be lost. I'd be a goner. He can do anything and everything, and all I can do is hold his hand.

As we emerge from the MacArthur BART station, we are assaulted by the sound of police sirens, the freeway rumbling above us, distant shouting. A man sells incense on the corner, the smoke heavy and suffocating. I don't want David to know I'm scared. This is a part of town we've never walked in, a part of town we never have any reason to visit. Dad says this part of town is for a different type of black people than us.

I have never been around so many black people in my life. We're the only ones in our neighborhood full of big, fancy houses. The only other people with brown skin are the guys mowing lawns and the women cleaning houses and taking care of babies. It is shocking to not feel so rare. I feel like I should know these people, that we must be related somehow. I feel left out.

I'm excited when a group of black boys approaches. They're closer to David's age than mine, but I know how to play with older kids. They're laughing, and I want to know what's so funny.

I want to laugh, too. But David is so serious. He tenses beside me; his hand grows tighter around mine. I pull his hand. "David," I say. He doesn't answer. He's looking straight ahead at the boys. "David."

"Look at those white boys," one of them yells, and they all laugh. I look behind us to see who he's talking to, but there's nobody there except the guy selling incense. David's arm tightens around me. His voice speaks low, "Walk faster, Marcus."

"Hey, I'm talking to you," the boy says. He's looking at us. "Come here. I want to ask you something."

"Keep walking," David says to me as we approach.

"Are you talking to us?" I say to the boy, all smiles. David always says I am too trusting.

Are you talking to us? the boy mimics in a high-pitched voice. The other boys laugh. I don't know what was so funny. I want to know what is funny. "Boy, you must be lost."

"Are we lost?" I ask David.

"Shut up, Marcus."

The boys make a wall in front of us with their bodies. They are not dressed like we are. Their skin is darker. Their shirts are white.

"Yeah, these motherfuckers are definitely lost," another boy says. "Look at those gay uniforms."

"You gotta pay the toll," says another.

Suddenly, I know I am supposed to be scared.

"You heard him, cracker," says the main one. He steps closer. His nose is inches from David's. "Pay the toll," he says. I wonder what his breath smells like. I wonder if it smells different from ours.

I don't know what I expect David to do, but I'm shocked when he steps forward and bumps the kid with his chest. The guy is at least four inches taller than David, but somehow David seems bigger.

"Oh, you want to fight, cracker?"

"I don't have to fight," David says with an eerie confidence. "You do, but I don't."

"What's this faggot talking about?" The kid laughs to his friends.

"Do you want to know why I don't have to fight? My father is the chief judge of the United States District Court for the Northern District of California. Who's your dad? Is he in prison? Do you even know who your father is?" David steps forward again, and the guy actually steps back, speechless. "If you fight me, your ass is going straight to jail. I'll say you attacked me. Who are the cops going to believe? Me and my brother, on our way home to Piedmont from private school, or some project niggers like you?"

Nobody speaks, nobody breathes. I close my eyes and hide behind David, my arms tight around him. We are on a busy street. Cars zoom by and people pass us on the sidewalk, but no one sees us. We are invisible.

When I open my eyes, the boys are gone. I don't look around to see where they are. I do not know if they spoke, if David spoke. I was somewhere else in those short moments, somewhere I couldn't hear anything but traffic and my own heart beating hard. I grab on tight to David's hand and focus on the sidewalk in front of me.

"Why'd you call them that?" I say after we've gone a few

blocks. "We're not supposed to say that word." He keeps walking. "Slow down, you're going too fast."

He turns around suddenly and grabs my shoulders, hard. "Listen to me, Marcus," he says, so serious it scares me. I start to cry. "You have to hit people where it hurts most. We're not tough, so we have to be smart. Do you hear me?"

"But why'd you have to call them that word?" I whimper. "Dad said we're never supposed to say that word."

"It's a bad word," David says, and I feel a little better with this confirmation. "The worst. You should never say it."

"Then why'd you say it?"

He sighs, and I know the world is so much heavier for him than it is for me. "You know how war works?" he says. "It's about showing superiority. They were winning, right? They're tougher than us. We can never beat them at their game. The only way we were going to win was if we change the game. That's called strategy. It's called psychological warfare. We have to make them small."

"Why?"

"So we win."

"But why?" I cry.

"Jesus, Marcus. So they won't kick our asses, that's why." He puts his arm around me and pulls me close. "You're going to have to learn how to take care of yourself someday. I'm not always going to be here to protect you."

"I can take care of myself," I say, wiping my wet nose on his sweater.

"I won't let anyone hurt you, little brother," David says. "I promise."

I believe him. I always believe him.

We walk the rest of the way home, not talking. When we finally make the turn that marks the official line between Oakland and the charter city of Piedmont where we live, things immediately feel different. Better. Safer. But even though the coast is clear, I keep my hand squeezed tight around David's. The flame of a tiny new terror ignites: I don't know how I'll ever be ready to let go.

here.

WHEN I GET HOME, I WANT NOTHING MORE THAN TO GRAB some food from the fridge and go to my room and listen to music, but Dad corners me in the kitchen. He's home at a time normal people get home from work, which is not normal for him. He's been doing this lately, being around. He actually ate lunch at the kitchen table on Saturday. He even knocked on my bedroom door a few nights ago to ask if I wanted to watch TV with him in the living room. I can't remember the last time he was even on my side of the house. I can't remember the last time someone even turned on the TV in the living room.

"How are you?" he says, with an unrecognizable smile. He's in khakis and his old Yale sweatshirt, and the clothes look strange on him. For the last several years, he's been someone who only looks right in a suit or his judge's robes. The last time I saw him in this ensemble was probably when I was a little kid, when he was still attempting to play the dad role. Before David started falling apart. Before Mom.

"Fine," I say, not meeting his eyes.

He puts his hand on my shoulder, and it makes me jump.

"I mean it, Marcus," he says. His face is softer than it should be. He's looking me in the eyes, like maybe he actually does want to know how I am. "You've been moping around the last few days. Is something wrong? Is something going on with that girl you've been seeing?"

"How'd you know I was seeing anyone?" He's never met Evie. He's never come close to meeting Evie.

"I notice things, Marcus."

I can't help but laugh. Bullshit.

"Have you thought about the internship at my office?"

"I've kind of had other things on my mind." That's the understatement of the year.

"I hope you'll at least consider it. It starts in two weeks. There are several applicants who are waiting anxiously for our response."

"So give it to one of them." I shake his hand off my shoulder.

"Marcus, it's a great opportunity. Not everybody gets a chance to work at the Supreme Court. It's quite a privilege. I hope you don't take that for granted."

Yes, Dad, I know. It's a privilege to have you as a father. Your expectations of me are a great fucking privilege.

"The internship will be impressive on your college applications. You are thinking about college, aren't you?"

"Of course I'm thinking about college," I say, gritting my teeth. "But I'm still a junior. I don't have to think about it too much yet."

"Some people would have already done some school visits and interviews by now. You've at least looked at some of those brochures, haven't you?"

He's talking about the pile of glossy pamphlets that has been collecting dust on the hallway table for the past few months, invitations from every college in the country that have gotten my name off some list that tells them I go to Templeton, which makes them drool for my family's money.

"Yeah, a little," I lie.

Dad sighs. Funny how he never worried about David.

I step toward the fridge. When I open it, I'm shocked to see real food—vegetables and fruits and ingredients for cooking, not the usual prepared meals and condiments. "You went shopping," I say.

"Monica and I went shopping. She's going to make us dinner tomorrow night. I want you to be here, Marcus."

I don't respond. He's been trying to get me to meet his current girlfriend for weeks, but I keep avoiding it. And now, more than ever, I don't want anything to do with her. I don't want any part in his trivial love life when mine is falling apart. I find an apple and a hunk of cheese in the fridge. I grab a box of crackers and a granola bar from the cabinet.

"I really want you to get to know her," he continues as I pretend to still be looking in the cabinet. I don't want to look at him right now. "You can't keep brushing her off. She means a lot to me. You mean a lot to me. I want you two to be friends."

I turn around in a rage. How can he be talking about this right now? Pretending his new bimbo of the month matters when the girl I'm in love with just got out of a fucking coma and isn't allowed to see me?

"Yeah, Dad," I say. "Sure, we can be friends. That totally makes sense since we're probably pretty close in age."

I expect a reaction. I want a reaction. I expect him to hit me, to yell, to at least storm away. But he just sighs. He just stands there. I want to hit him. I want to knock that smug look off his face. But he is, and always will be, so much bigger than me.

"I guess I deserve that," he says, then emits a strange sound. If he were anyone else, I'd say it was a chuckle. "But for your information, Monica is forty-four and CEO of a successful tech start-up that's about to go public." He seems to register the look on my face that says this news means nothing to me. "I'm serious about this one," he says.

"Congratulations, Dad," I say, and I walk away.

there.

THE DINING ROOM IS A MUSEUM, A PLACE FULL OF THINGS no one touches. But tonight is special, Mom says. It's Dad's birthday. The kitchen is a war zone, bombs of flour exploded on counters, floor, walls. Measuring spoons and cups thrown around. Boxes and cans and jars in disarray.

We are sitting at the dining room table. Mom dressed us up. David kicks me under the table for pulling at the neck of my sweater vest. "It's scratchy," I whine.

"Shhh," he says, but I don't know why we have to be quiet. It's just us three. Mom's sitting way over on the other end of the table, her face pale under her makeup.

"Mommy, you look pretty," David says.

She smiles, but it is her own special sad kind of smile. "Thank you, honey."

"When is Dad coming home?" I say. David kicks me again, but I don't know why. He knows so many things I don't, like when to talk and when not to talk. Like when Mom is sad or Dad is angry, even when no one is talking.

Mom says nothing. We've been sitting here for a long time. My stomach tells me we should have eaten by now. The food is in the fancy bowls we only use on holidays, covered by matching lids. There's no way it can still be warm.

There's a cake in the kitchen, a surprise. Mom made it from scratch. David and I watched YouTube videos with her about how to make flowers out of frosting.

"You boys must be starving." She sighs. "Why don't you make yourself a couple of plates and take them upstairs?"

"Are you sure?" David asks.

"We can eat in our rooms?" I say. "Like, while we play video games?"

"Just for tonight," she says with a weak smile. "It's a special occasion."

David sits next to me in the back of Dad's car, arms crossed on his chest, his face pinched in an angry pout. I don't know what he's so upset about. Most boys would jump at the chance to shoot a real gun.

We drive by the sign for the Chabot Gun Club. "Here we are," Dad says from the front seat. I can't remember the last time we did something, just the three of us. I want David to be as excited as I am.

I follow Dad to the front desk, David trailing behind. "I have a lane reserved for one thirty," Dad says. "Bill Lyon." As he fills out forms, I look around. Out the window, many of the lanes are occupied by people like us—fathers teaching sons how to shoot. Half a dozen old men sit on a bench and folding chairs near the front desk, as if this is a living room, comfortable in a way that implies they've been sitting there for a long time. David is still near the entrance, looking at a glass cabinet full of old pictures and trophies.

"I tell you," says one of the old men, in a raspy smoker's voice, "this is the only place left in the whole Bay Area where the Second Amendment is still alive and well."

"Yep," says another.

"This town sure has gone to shit."

"Uh-huh," says another.

"What with all the bike lanes and gay marriage."

They all nod their heads in agreement.

Dad hands me a pair of plastic safety goggles. I feel a little less tough than I was hoping to.

"I don't want to wear those," David says.

"You have to," Dad says. "It's the rules."

"I don't see what the point is if I'm not even going to touch a gun."

"David," Dad says in his taking-no-bullshit tone, "put the goggles on now." He so rarely talks to David that way, it makes me feel uneasy, like the world is suddenly tilted in the wrong direction.

David takes the goggles and follows us out the door to our lane under the wooden shelter of the handgun range. He's got his arms crossed on his chest. "America's obsession with guns is so screwed up," he says, but Dad ignores him. "Did you know that every day, eighty-eight Americans are killed by gun violence? Did you know that every month, forty-eight women are shot and killed by domestic abusers? Did you know that American kids are sixteen times more likely to accidentally be shot and killed than kids in other developed countries?"

"How do you even know that?" I say, but David ignores me.

"I hate guns," he says as Dad sets a black wooden box down on a small table. "I don't want to touch a gun. I don't want to fire a gun. I don't want anything to do with guns. And I'm ashamed and appalled that you think so highly of them."

"Oh, get off your high horse, David. You're fourteen years old. You know nothing about the world." Dad opens the box and inside is a shiny silver old-fashioned revolver. It's the first time I've ever seen a gun in real life, besides on a police officer. And I'm going to get to touch it. I'm going to shoot it. Dad is going to show me how. He thinks I'm big enough.

"A fourteen-year-old is smart enough to know that guns kills people," David says. "In fact, guns kill fourteen-year-olds all the time."

"David, shut up!" I say. I am not going to let him ruin this for me. A girl in the lane next to us giggles. Her boyfriend has his arms around her, showing her how to hold his gun.

"Just touch it," I say. "It's not going to hurt you."

He pokes at the gun with his finger, then pulls it away as if burned.

"Be a man, David," Dad says. "Men know how to handle guns."

"Maybe I don't want to be your version of a man," he grumbles under his breath, and Dad pretends not to hear.

"Do you want to be a woman?" I say, trying to make him laugh, but he rolls his eyes at me, slumps into a plastic chair, and takes out his phone and starts poking at it.

Dad tears the phone out of David's hand and shoves it in his pocket. "You are going to pay attention," he growls. "You are going to learn how to do this."

Birds chirp. The trees of the Berkeley hills surround us. On the other side of this patch of forest, people are golfing and hiking and having picnics. They can probably hear the guns going off. If a deer walked into the shooting range, I wonder if we'd be allowed to shoot it.

As Dad shows us the boring stuff—how to clean the gun, how to load it, how the safety works—I try to ignore David sulking beside me. He's like a sponge, sucking out my joy and excitement. When it's finally time to shoot, I feel strangely sad. This day is nothing like I'd hoped it would be.

I'm a terrible shot. I had imagined myself as some kind of action hero in a flashy movie, but I'm a kid in a run-down old shooting range who, after several rounds, only hits the target once, on the very edge of the paper.

After everyone's done shooting, the ranger announces the cease-fire and I walk down the lane to replace the target I hit. I roll up the piece of paper with one tiny hole in it, careful not to get any creases in it. I will put it in the box where I keep my most treasured possessions. When I return, Dad looks at his watch. "Time's almost up," he says. "One last chance, David."

David sits there for a while, silent and still, in his own little world. I load the gun for myself, expecting David to keep pouting until it's time to leave.

But then he stands up. He says, "Okay." He walks over to me and pulls the loaded gun out of my hand. He turns to face the target. He raises the gun, aims, and shoots the six bullets in quick succession. They all hit the target, one just shy of a bull's-eye.

"Wow," I say.

"Ha!" Dad exclaims with joy. He pounds David on the back with fatherly pride. "That's my kid genius. That's my big man."

David winces and says nothing. I've never seen him look so small.

you.

YOU HADN'T SEEN ME YET. I WAS SURE THE LOUD RUM-bling of my car's diesel engine would give me away, but you were in your own world, looking up at the sky like you didn't quite trust it. I thought, How is it possible for one face to tell so many stories and at the same time divulge nothing? You were a beautiful mystery I wanted to solve.

I parked my car at the corner. I whispered, "Look at me," and even though it was impossible that you heard me, you turned and looked me straight in the eyes. Like you knew exactly where my eyes were, these two gray-green pinpricks in the distance, like magnets. In that moment, my suspicions were confirmed: we were connected on a level that betrayed all laws of space and time and sound.

We had barely kissed yet, but when you got into the car, I wanted to inhale you, I wanted to taste every piece of you. It wasn't just a sex thing, wasn't just my body's hunger for yours.

I wanted to know you with every single one of my senses. I wanted inside. I wanted everything. I wanted your molecules.

It shocked me that you existed in the same world as other girls I've known. You were nothing like the prep school girls I met at Templeton parties, those girls with the swishing ponytails and easy laughs, their eyes warmed with vodka and entitlement as they curled up against me. You were nothing like the hipster girls I met at music shows, those spindly-armed poets who drank cheap beer as proof of their authenticity, who caressed my skin and laughed ironically about how white they were, who called me beautiful as if I were some kind of exotic art piece. You were something else entirely. Your identity was not theoretical, not a performance, not a role. You were the real deal.

Your beauty was transcendent. The sky spun in your eyes. Maybe because you had tasted death and brought a little of it back with you, maybe because you had brushed hands with God, you looked and felt and tasted like heaven.

And now this hell. Life without you. A vacuum, a black hole.

here.

I KEEP PICTURING EVIE IN THE HOSPITAL, LYING IN ONE OF those beds she hated, alone and scared. No matter how hard I try to think of something else, I keep seeing her there, I keep seeing myself with her, and everything in my body wants to be there, to wrap her up and take her away, and the impossibility of it all makes me crazy. She's on the other side of town, locked up in a tower that I can't climb, guarded by people who won't let me see her, by parents who think I'm the reason she's in there. But I'm the one who saved her. I'm the one who wants to save her still.

It does no good wondering about the past, wishing I could change it. But I can't help hating myself for not noticing the signs that she was in trouble. Those far-off looks she'd get. How she'd disappear sometimes when she was sitting right next to me. How she kept wanting to get higher and higher, how she was never high enough. I keep thinking I should have loved her better somehow.

I should have said something sooner. Maybe there was a way I could have saved her from this.

I can't do anything about the past, but I can do something about now. I can find my way back to her. I can save us.

I am on my way to the coffee shop where we met for our first date. I remember being so nervous I changed my outfit five times before I got in my car to meet her. She was unlike any girl I had ever met—so real, so *authentic*—I didn't want her to think I was just another high school idiot. I wanted her to think I was cool enough, smart, funny. I wanted her to think I was worthy.

Before Evie, I had made a habit of not getting close to anyone. It was my code. Don't get close and no one can hurt you. They can't use you. They can't let you down. They can't leave. But something about Evie made me go against my code. Something about her convinced me she was worth the risk.

So now here I am, standing in the same spot where a few short weeks ago I tried not to stutter as I attempted witty banter with Evie. Here are all the hip people sitting around, poking at computers, and eating overpriced toast. I take a deep breath as I step up to the counter. The short, androgynous guy at the counter looks at me with confused recognition and pauses a moment before smiling and saying, "What can I get you?" For a moment, I consider running.

"Hi," I say, and it comes out sounding like a frog croaking.

"Hi," he says, his smile wavering. Maybe he thinks I'm going to steal the tip jar.

"I don't know if you remember me," I begin. "You probably

don't. I came here a few weeks ago with Evie Whinsett." His smile immediately fades into a look of pure sadness. "Um . . . she's kind of in trouble right now and I can't get a hold of her, and I guess I figured you know her, so I wanted to talk to you to, you know, see if you could help me or, I don't know. Shit, I'm sorry. I'm probably not making any sense."

"It's okay," he says with a small smile. "I'm off in half an hour. Can you wait until then?"

"Yes, of course. Thank you."

I wander around Telegraph Avenue for the next thirty minutes, trying to busy my mind with window-shopping so I don't have to think about Evie, but she breaks through everything. Here's the yoga studio ("Fifteen dollars to do some stretching for an hour?" Evie would say. "Ridiculous"). Here's the tattoo shop (I wonder what kind of tattoo Evie would get. Something pretty and botanical, I bet. But not predictable. A weed, maybe. A dandelion). Here's the Burmese restaurant (Evie's favorite). Here's the organic ice cream shop with the weird flavors (another of Evie's favorites). She's everywhere, in everything.

The half hour is excruciating. When I get back to the coffee shop, Evie's friend is counting the money out of the tip jar. I catch his eye and he smiles, and I remember the first time I saw him, how he looked so happy to see Evie, but she seemed almost scared, how she went outside to talk to him in private and returned, shaken, desperate to leave the café. She told me nothing and I didn't push it. I was so wrapped up in my insecurities and expectations, I didn't even notice how weird it was.

"Let's get a doughnut," he says, and I follow him out the door.

"I'm Cole," he says as we walk down Telegraph and into the alley full of tiny, expensive boutiques. A window displays a red flannel shirt for $250 ("Try it on!" Evie would say, and we'd laugh about how the five-dollar thrift store flannel I'm already wearing looks so much better).

"I'm Marcus," I say.

"Are you Evie's new boyfriend?" he asks.

"Yes," I say. "Wait. *New* boyfriend? Is there an old boyfriend?"

He looks at me with kindness in his eyes that borders too close to pity.

"Let's go in here," he says, and leads me into a tiny shop displaying four flavors of crème-filled artisanal doughnuts. Cole orders a chocolate-hazelnut and a vanilla-persimmon flavored one, and I order a raspberry one even though I am in no mood to eat.

"She had a lot of secrets," I say, like an apology. Cole nods as we sit on a bench outside.

"So what's up?" he says as he bites into a doughnut. "How's Evie?"

"She's in the hospital."

He swallows. "Shit," he says, shaking his head. "The cancer's back?"

"No, she had an accident. Swimming."

"Is she okay?"

"She was in a coma for a day. But she's awake now. At least that's what I've been told. I haven't seen her. It's a long story, but her parents aren't my biggest fans."

"So you're contacting me to see if I can help you see her."

"Yeah. Yes. I guess that's what I'm doing."

"I'm sorry," he says, looking genuinely sorry. "I wish I could help you, but I don't really have any idea how to contact her. We weren't close. I just met her once, actually." He's quiet for a moment as he stares at his doughnut. He's gone somewhere far away. "She was my girlfriend's friend. My ex-girlfriend. Fuck," he says, setting the doughnut down on his lap. "What do you call it when your girlfriend dies?"

"I don't know," I say, but it is a stupid thing to say. Cole wasn't asking for an answer.

"Stella loved Evie like crazy," he says. "I was a little jealous, actually. Stella liked girls, too, and Evie was beautiful. But you already knew that."

I'm not sure if I nod. I'm not sure what any part of my body is doing.

"But it wasn't like that," Cole continues. "I think what Stella loved was Evie's sweetness. Her innocence, you know? How she was this little blond cheerleader with the football player boyfriend and perfect family, but she wasn't stuck up about it or anything. She was so generous with her love. So open."

My head is spinning. The ground has been pulled out from under me and I am falling through space and there is nothing and no one to catch me. Who the hell is he talking about? Not Evie. Not the Evie I know.

He seems to sense my shock. "You're surprised by some of this?"

"Yeah. Pretty much all of it, to be honest."

"I guess she changed a lot after she got out of the hospital."

"That would be an understatement."

"Makes sense, really. She went through a lot. She almost died, then didn't. Then her really close friend died. That'll change anyone."

We sit there in silence for a while. Cole picks up his doughnut and continues eating.

"She was a cheerleader?" It's the only thing I can think of saying.

Cole laughs, which loosens the vise grip on my heart. He looks me up and down, at my boots and ripped jeans, my faded thrift store T-shirt and short dreadlocks. "Not quite your usual type?"

"Not really."

"Yeah, not Stella's either. But Evie was special, I guess."

"Is special. She *is* special."

"Sorry."

"It's okay."

"I have to go to class," Cole says, standing up. "Been working since eight this morning—now I have to go to three hours of night class. Good times."

"Thanks for talking to me," I say.

"Sorry I couldn't be more helpful. I probably made it worse, huh?"

I look up at him and try to smile. "Yeah, kind of."

He reaches out his hand and we shake. "Take care of yourself," Cole says, and walks away.

I sit there for a few minutes, trying to imagine the tough girl I know as a cheerleader, in one of those ridiculous outfits they wear, jumping around with pom-poms, squealing for a football game, or parading through the halls of her high school on the arm of a dumb jock. I can't help but laugh, and it's the laughter that saves me, even as I attract a few strange looks, even as a couple people scoot a little farther away from me on the bench. It's the laughter that keeps me from screaming.

you.

I TOLD YOU VIRTUALLY NOTHING ABOUT MY MOM, ABOUT David. Even though you were the first person I ever wanted to talk to, even though I wanted to pour myself into you. But I knew it would scare you. So I tried to give you myself in little pieces. Certain things had to wait, big things. It never seemed like the right time for those. Something else was going on. You were always upset about something, and it took up your whole world, our whole world. So I told myself, next time. But next time never came.

I know there were things you wanted to tell me, but maybe you didn't feel the same ripping inside your chest as I did whenever you kept silent. Maybe you were at peace with your secrets. Maybe they didn't tear you apart. Maybe all that chemo and radiation that racked your body before I met you made your heart radioactive, made it hard and indestructible.

No, you can't fool me. You're as soft inside as I am. I know this because I love you. I know this because you did let me in long enough for my heart to get comfortable, long enough to know it was somewhere I belonged.

And now I yearn for that softness inside you. It is somewhere far away from me, guarded by secrets and distance and fear. You are a coward, Evie. Your silence makes you a coward. Did you think I wouldn't hear you? Did you think your truth would not find a home outside your walls? How could you have not known I was listening? The whole time, waiting for you to speak. The whole time, making a home to keep your secrets safe.

I should have tried harder. I should have done more to pull the truth out of you. I was a coward, too. But that ends now. I refuse to lose you. I will not give up that easily. I will not let you drift away and pretend you did not leave some pieces of you with me.

I want to tell you the truth. I want to tell you everything.

there.

MOM IS SITTING IN THE KITCHEN, LOOKING INTO SPACE, completely still, as if she's trying to hide in plain sight, like deer that freeze when they hear a noise, hoping their stillness will make them invisible. I have never seen anyone so alone.

"Where's Dad?" I say, and the air shakes with the sudden sound of my voice. I swear I hear the walls rattle.

"Who knows?" she says without looking at me, with a new edge to her voice that sounds wrong, like it doesn't belong there. There is something sad, something embarrassing, about the clothes she is wearing—tight black leggings that may not actually qualify as pants, a shirt that hangs so low on her shoulders I can see both bra straps.

"Shouldn't *you* know?" I say.

Her head snaps in my direction, a sudden flurry of movement, and now I am the deer, caught, frozen in the headlights coming way too fast in my direction. "Get out!" she shouts, and she is the car speeding toward me, and I know I'm supposed to move, but my instincts are wrong, they're not letting me move, they want me to stay, to be with her.

"Why?" I say.

"Marcus, go to your room."

I don't move.

"I don't want you here."

I tell my feet to go, but they won't.

"Leave me alone!"

And then I do the exact opposite of what I'm supposed to. I start walking toward her, my socked feet sliding across the floor, my body pushing against the force of a magnet turned backward. The closer I get, the stronger it gets, the invisible push of her rejection.

Then a coffee cup flies through the air. I feel its trajectory against my cheek, the displaced molecules of air as it misses hitting my face. Then the smash, an explosion behind me.

Then the stillness again. Mom's eyes back in her nowhere place. Her backward magnet so strong it pushes me out the door and up the stairs, into my room so far, far away.

Mom and David are in the living room. They don't know I am here. I am trying to understand David's special access to Mom, why she is more his than mine.

She is on her second bottle of wine. She pours him a glass and they say "Cheers." This is their special time, their bonding time.

She says, "Tell me everything," and he does. He tells her things he doesn't even tell me—grown-up things, stuff about his girlfriend, about sex, about feeling lost and weak and uninspired. She sits with her legs crossed on her favorite oversized comfy chair, and he lies on the couch, as if she is a therapist and he is her patient. I have watched this scene before. I have watched Mom shine in the glow of being needed. But also something else, almost like she's bribing him, like she's buying his attention and time with the wine, like she doesn't trust him to want to stick around without some kind of incentive.

Tonight they exchange places. Mom finishes the second bottle of wine and starts talking. "Your father doesn't appreciate me," she says, slurring her words slightly. "My only job is to get dressed up and be charming at his important functions." The back of David's head nods. "I have my own dreams, you know," Mom says. "Dreams your dad doesn't give a shit about and are never going to come true as long as I'm married to him."

She lifts her wineglass and tries to take a sip, but it is empty. She sets it back down on the coffee table, disgusted. "I think I'm going to leave your father," she says. "I'll take you with me."

"What about Marcus?" David says.

She says nothing. I cannot read her face. She is staring into space, into nowhere. She is already gone.

My insides liquefy. I am dizzy, sick. If she ever answers the question, I do not know. I do not wait to find out. I walk up the stairs, the sound of my footsteps muted by my dirty white socks.

I lie in bed, looking at the glow-in-the-dark stars on my ceiling that David helped me configure into real constellations. I push the thoughts out of my head of what life would be like without them in it, if I was left in this big house with no one but Dad.

here.

AS SOON AS I WALK THROUGH THE FRONT DOOR OF MY house, I know something is wrong. It smells weird, and it takes me a few moments to realize it's the scent of something cooking. But even stranger are the sounds coming out of the kitchen—something I barely recognize as my father's laughter and someone else's, a woman's.

I'm not sure what I expected to see when I opened the door, but it definitely wasn't my dad being spoon-fed sauce by a woman who looks closer to his age than anyone he's ever dated. She's black, too, which is a first. Dad's dated two women since my mom left, both briefly, both in their twenties, one white and one Filipina, I think. Or maybe Vietnamese. She wasn't around long enough for me to find out.

"You must be Marcus!" the woman says.

"Hey," I say. I meet Dad's eyes for a second and am shocked to see them wrinkled in a smile.

"This is Monica," he says. "My girlfriend." He sounds so proud of himself, almost giddy, like he's suddenly thirteen instead of fifty-two.

"It's so great to finally meet you," she says, stepping forward and shaking my hand with the one not holding the spoon. "I hope you'll join us for dinner. I made polenta cakes with sausage and peppers."

"Monica's a great cook," Dad says as he puts his arm around her waist. "She spent her junior year of college in Florence." She turns her head and kisses him on the cheek, and he laughs, and this is too weird. Even being alone with my crazy thoughts is better than being subjected to this.

"I already ate," I lie. I still have the doughnut I bought this afternoon in my bag. That will have to be my dinner tonight. No way I'm coming back down here. "I have homework."

"Oh, darn," Monica says. *Darn*? Who says *darn*? "Well, next time."

"Yeah, whatever," I say.

Her smile cracks a little, and I'm surprised I feel bad about being so rude. It's not her fault my dad's an asshole. She hasn't known him long enough.

"Marcus," Dad says in his judge voice. I wonder if Monica can hear the undertones of hostility, the potential for rage. "Monica worked really hard on this meal. I've been promising her dinner with you for weeks now."

"It's okay, William," she says. "Really. We can do it another time."

William? His name is Bill, lady.

"Fine," he says. I wonder if she notices the look in my father's eyes, the one that says *I'm going to kill you.* "Another time."

"It was really nice meeting you, Marcus," she says. "I'm looking forward to getting to know you." She looks me in the eyes as she says this, and I know in that moment that my dad is in fact serious about her, and she's serious about him. Maybe he has moved on. Maybe he isn't still settling for vague versions of my mother, when she was young and beautiful and eager to please, and he assumed that's all she was.

"Yeah," I say. "You, too." And I'm not sure I don't mean it. As I walk out of the kitchen and up to my room, the floor feels somehow different under my feet, softer and less stable. The walls feel warped. The shadows in the corner are too many shades of gray.

there.

IT IS SATURDAY MORNING. OTHER FAMILIES ARE JUST GET-
ting up. They are still in their pajamas, in warm kitchens that
smell like coffee and pancakes. But in our house, Dad is heading
out the door for work. He has been promoted. He is too important
to stay home.

He thinks he can sneak out without us noticing. He doesn't
know I'm at my hidden perch at the top of the stairs. He doesn't
know Mom is waking up at this very moment. He didn't notice
her curled up on her chair in the living room. He doesn't know
she's been there since last night; they've had separate bedrooms for
nearly a year.

Maybe she has already started drinking this morning. Maybe
she is still drunk from the night before. She is on the floor now,
hanging off him, pulling on his coat, trying to keep him from
walking out the door. She is crying and I can understand only
half of what she's saying. The only thing I'm sure of is that I can't

un-see any of this. I cannot un-feel this embarrassment, this com-bination of sadness and disgust. I want to look away, but I can't.

Mom is on her knees, her face blotchy and wet with tears. She cries, "You're going to see her, aren't you?"

My father looks down at her coldly, his dark brown skin so smooth and untroubled, as if he cannot be bothered by her antics. The scene looks like something out of a play, staged for ultimate dramatic effect, my father and mother actors cast as husband and wife, but who barely know each other in real life. The contrast between them is so great. The contrast is all they are.

I wonder in this moment who I resemble more—my mother or my father. I am undeniably black, though I am much lighter than Dad. My hair is kinky like his, but I have Mom's green eyes and straight nose, am thin and lanky like her, not stocky and broad shouldered like Dad. But then there are the other, deeper traits. Am I the serious, driven, unfeeling man towering above my mother, or the needy and erratic woman on the floor next to him?

I feel David slide next to me at the top of the stairs. We sit there for a moment, listening to Mom beg, listening to Dad bark, "Renae, pull yourself together. This is pathetic."

David puts his arm around me. He says, "Let's get the fuck out of here."

Our parents don't notice us come down the stairs. We walk right past them, through the kitchen, and out the back door, and we drive away in Bubbles, David's new vintage Mercedes station wagon, not talking, not needing to talk.

I know where we are headed as soon as we get off the freeway, even though it has been a few years since Mom has taken us there.

We sit on a piece of driftwood, the beach empty except for a couple of seagulls. David pulls out a pipe and fills it with sticky green herb, lights it with a lighter, and inhales. He hands the pipe to me and I put it to my lips, giddy to be joining him in this secret. It feels like some sort of initiation into manhood, like our dysfunctional family's weird version of a bar mitzvah. David puts up his hand to block the wind, lights the bowl for me, and I inhale and cough, surprised that the smoke does not taste minty. We pass the pipe back and forth until all we have left is ash. David blows and it floats away on the wind, breaks into particles, smaller and smaller, and is swallowed into the bay.

I don't know if I'm high, but I know something is different. I am sitting next to my brother and we are somewhere no one can find us. Mom probably forgot this place exists. Now David and I have something that is just ours. In a couple of months, summer will be over and I will finally be a freshman at Templeton with him, a senior. David and I will share the same world. He will take up the space where I hold my worries. He will be so big, he will crowd everything else out.

"I don't feel anything," I say.

"You will," David says, looking out across the water. He picks up a rock and throws it. "And then none of this shit will matter."

here.

I DON'T KNOW WHAT I EXPECTED TO FIND, BUT I WENT BACK
to the beach. Maybe I thought there'd be a clue. Or maybe I
thought the clothes Evie took off before she entered the water
would still be there, piled on a piece of driftwood, her phone
charged and tucked safely in her pocket. Maybe I thought they
would be untouched, unbothered by human hands or the weather,
that I could bury my nose in her shirt and still smell her. But every
sign of Evie was gone. Someone had probably thrown away her
clothes, taken her cash and whatever else they could use out of her
wallet, and hacked her phone to sell. The beach was just a beach,
covered by rocks and seaweed and what seemed like more garbage
than usual.

I found nothing. I am running out of ideas. So now here I am
again, waiting for Evie's sister outside her school, even though she
made it clear that she wasn't interested in seeing me again. But I
have to know how Evie's doing, and after trying the hospital and

Cole, this is the only thing I can think of besides going to her house.

"You again?" a sharp voice says behind me, and I turn around to find Jenica.

"How is she?"

Jenica sighs. "You can't keep doing this."

"I don't have a choice."

"You could choose to leave us alone."

"That's not an option."

"You know my parents hate you, right? They're never going to let you see her." I open my mouth to protest, but she keeps talking. "They think you got Evie hooked on drugs. They wanted to press charges, but she convinced them not to."

My heart jumps. Evie was thinking about me. Talking about me. Defending me. I still exist.

"We smoked a little pot, that's all," I say, only partly lying. "We drank a little." She was drunk when I left her that afternoon, but that was all her doing. I left her at home, where she was safe. I didn't know she would go back to the beach. I didn't know she'd go swimming.

Jenica blinks and says nothing, and I'm not sure if she believes me, if she's convinced of my innocence.

"Did you tell her to call me?"

"She couldn't even if she wanted to. She got sent straight to rehab as soon as she got released from the hospital. The only people she's allowed to call are my parents."

"Rehab?" I say. "For smoking pot and drinking?"

Jenica stares at me for a long time and I can't quite read the look on her face. "You don't know?" she finally says, and her face softens with a wave of emotion. It could be compassion. It could be pity.

"I don't know what?"

"Oh, wow."

"I don't know *what*?"

What else didn't Evie tell me? Is there anything real about the girl I fell in love with?

"She had a ton of opiates in her system when you brought her to the ER," Jenica says.

"What?" I say. "Opiates? What are you talking about?" I wonder for a moment if we're talking about the same person, if there's another Evie who goes to North Berkeley High who has a sister named Jenica.

"She had a problem with pain pills after she got out of the hospital the last time, but we thought she was over it. She promised. God, we were so stupid."

I'm trying to wrap my head around this timeline. Evie was on pills after she got out of the hospital, *before* she met me. That means she must have been on pills the whole time we were together.

I cannot feel my body. I am incapable of feeling. If I feel just a little, the floodgates will open and I'll be destroyed. Did Evie tell me the truth about anything?

"Wow, you really didn't know," Jenica says. "I actually feel sorry for you. Well, get in line. Yours is not the first heart she's broken. You know Evie had a boyfriend when she started seeing you, right? And she was stringing you both along?"

I don't say anything. My mind is stopped, frozen. It cannot process this nightmare of information.

"His name is Will. They'd been together for two years. He stayed by her side the whole time she had cancer. He came to visit her in the hospital almost every day." Jenica is agitated, angry. Her voice is shaking. "What'd *you* do? Get her high? Share some of your drugs with her?"

I don't want to hear this. I can't. "I need to talk to her," I say.

"She doesn't want to talk to you."

She's lying. She has to be lying. "There has to be a way for her to call me."

"Dude, I'm serious. She doesn't want to talk to you. *I* don't want to talk to you. It's over. Give up. Leave us alone."

I grab her arm as she starts walking away. I need something, anything, solid in my hand. "Don't touch me!" she snaps, and pulls away. I let her go, and I wonder if that's the last piece of Evie I will ever touch.

you.

I KNEW SOMETHING WAS WRONG THAT NIGHT WE SLEPT on the beach. Part of you was gone, replaced by a stranger who only cared about getting high. I tried to get you to talk—about your family, your friends, the cancer, anything—but you were closed up so tight I felt like I was scraping at concrete with my fingernails. You finally gave a little, but you stayed so vague, giving me tears but no details. And then you kissed me, as if a kiss would wipe away your sadness, as if it would distract me from my mission to discover the source of it. And it did. And that shames me.

The next night, you were even worse. It's like you were becoming transparent, threadbare. I had the feeling you were going to disappear any second. I didn't want to get high, didn't want that to be the only thing that brought us together, but I smoked with you anyway because I knew you'd do it without me, even as I sat there next to you, and I couldn't bear to see you getting high alone.

Had we ever been sober together? I can't even remember.

It felt so familiar. Your distance and my desperate yearning to reach you. The feeling of running and running and never getting any closer. You were so much like David, so lost to me. I could feel you going down the same road as he did. I could feel myself following you. And even though you were there with me, even though our bodies were touching, I suddenly felt so alone. And being lonely when you're with someone is the worst kind of loneliness.

I was so torn when you threw yourself at me. My body wanted you. God, how it wanted you. But my heart wanted something else, wanted the part of you that hid inside your body. I could tell you weren't really there. The light was gone in your eyes, replaced by something dark, frantic, terrified. I know it wasn't me you wanted in that moment. You wanted the distraction of my body. You wanted to use me like a drug. You wanted my body to get you high.

As hard as it was, I managed to say no. I know you were hurt by my refusal. You thought it meant I didn't want you. How could I possibly explain how untrue that is? How could you not see that my stopping was proof of how much I love you?

there.

"DOES THIS LOOK OKAY?" I SAY. I AM ON MY FOURTH OUT-fit. I am going to my first Templeton party with David. There will be girls there. They are the only thing I think about. "Do I look old enough?"

"Old enough for what?" David says as he reaches behind his dresser and pulls out a hidden pack of cigarettes and a small bottle of vodka. It doesn't surprise me anymore when he does things like this. In the last few months, we've gotten drunk and smoked pot together plenty of times. I don't know how long he's been doing this or how much he does it without me. I don't know if he's doing anything stronger. All I know is how I feel when he shares it with me, like I am part of his world, like he wants me in it, like he is not drifting away and becoming someone I don't know.

I unbutton my plaid flannel shirt for the second time. "Old enough for a girl to want to kiss me."

David laughs and hands me the bottle. "Here, drink some of this. Liquid courage."

It burns and tastes like poison, but I swallow because David is always right.

"Are the girls from Saint Catherine's hot?"

"The hottest," David says. "You know what they say about Catholic school girls."

I don't, but I nod anyway. "Do you think any of them will make out with me?"

"Not if you say dumb shit like that."

I button the shirt back up. "Which way looks better?"

"Dude," David says. "You look fine. If you take any longer, I'm going to change my mind about letting you come with me."

"Wait," I say.

"Jesus, Marcus. What?"

My face burns with my question. I look at my feet, at the wall, at the bed, anywhere besides in my brother's eyes.

"Marcus, I am this close to leaving without you. Spit it out."

"How do you make a girl have sex with you?"

I expect him to laugh his ass off, but he doesn't. He's quiet for a long time. He's thinking way too hard.

"Never mind," I say. "Let's go."

"No," he says. "Sit down for a second."

I sit on David's bed and he sits next to me. I expect a lecture about not saying the first thing I think of, of having a better filter. We've had this talk before.

"Marcus, listen to me," he says. "You know you can't *make* a girl have sex with you. It's not like that."

"I know," I said, but I don't. I have no idea what he's talking about. I have no idea why he's so serious.

"You know that's not all they're for, right? Being hot and having sex with?"

I roll my eyes. The longer we sit here, the more I feel like a little, stupid kid.

"I'm serious," David says. "I know what it's like going to all-boys schools your whole life. It fucks with your head. It's not natural."

"I'm not an idiot, David."

"I know," he says. He's quiet for a minute. "It's not just that."

"What?"

He hands me the bottle and I hold my breath as I take another swig, as I feel the fire burn down my throat. David takes a huge swig and doesn't even flinch.

"Don't ever treat a girl the way Dad treats Mom," he says. "Don't let them love you and not love them back."

I want to think I don't know what he's talking about. In that moment, I want to be young for a change. I want to be innocent and dumb and clueless. I want girls to remain soft, pretty, untouchable things. Not future women, not mothers and wives. Not people who can get hurt.

I am not as excited about the party as I was before. The night is still full of possibility, but now also danger. Also things that cannot be undone.

"No, Marcus," David says as he pulls a black sweatshirt over his head. "I told you already. You can't come."

Not even a year has passed, and David has turned into someone different. Not even a year, and I am turning into nothing.

"Why not?"

He doesn't answer. He's looking in his wallet, frowning. "Hey, do you have a twenty I can borrow?"

"If you let me come with you."

He sighs and shakes his head. He starts opening the drawers of his dresser, searching behind socks and T-shirts for forgotten stashes of money. It's Friday night and I don't want to spend it alone. Besides David, there's no one else I hang out with.

I pull out my wallet and hand him a twenty-dollar bill. He doesn't even meet my eyes as he takes it and crams it into his pocket.

"So can I come with you now?" I say.

He looks at me in a way that makes me shrivel. He starts walking out his bedroom door.

"Why not? You have to at least give me a reason."

David sighs and faces me, irritated, like I'm a waste of his time. "Things are different now. I'm doing different things."

"But I'm different. I can be different."

"I don't want you to be different." What he means is, I'm leaving you behind.

"Just give me a chance, okay? I won't embarrass you or anything, I promise."

"Dammit, Marcus. I said no. What part of no don't you

80

fucking understand? You're not coming with me."

I am no one.

He's a shadow. That's what he is. Not David. Not my brother. Just a shadow as he walks out the door.

I wake to Mom shaking me.

"Marcus," she says through the clouds. "Come on. Get dressed. We have to go."

"Why?" I mumble.

"David was in an accident." Her voice breaks. My eyes burst open and let in way too much light. "He's in the hospital. We have to go."

When we get to the hospital, David is barely awake. He got lucky with just a broken rib and a few stitches. He stares out at me through the haze of painkillers and tries to smile. Something is missing behind his eyes. But his face is relaxed, serene. He looks the calmest I've seen him in years.

"Little brother," he mumbles. "Your turn."

"What are you talking about? My turn for what?"

But he is gone, sucked into oblivion. And somewhere, deep down, I know he's never coming back.

I wanted to go with him tonight. I was supposed to be with him.

I am in the kitchen, searching for food. Mom hasn't gone grocery shopping in days. She hasn't bothered to pay someone else to do it for her. There is one frostbitten egg roll in the freezer. I throw it in the microwave. I listen to the soft buzz as it cooks. I bet David could explain the science about how exactly microwaves work if he wasn't so busy fighting with Dad.

The house is big and the walls are thick, but I can still hear them screaming at each other. I don't know what the fight is about this time. They all melt into each other. Maybe it's the DUI. Or the getting caught with cocaine at school. Or the possibility of Yale taking back his acceptance. Or getting that girl pregnant and asking Dad for money for the abortion. The fight could be about anything and everything David does these days, his senior year of high school, when his life was supposed to look so different.

"What the hell were you thinking?" Dad screams.

"Why is my life any of your business?" David screams back.

"You call this a life?"

Over and over, around and around, these demands and questions that neither ever answers.

I wrap the egg roll in a paper towel and walk out of the kitchen. Mom is sitting in her favorite chair in the living room, a book in one hand, a giant glass of wine in the other. Her face is pointed in the direction of the book, but she's not actually reading. Her eyes are glazed over, focused on nothing.

"Mom," I say. She says nothing. She doesn't move. "Mom!" I say again, louder. Her eyelids flicker, she blinks, and she's back, but just barely.

"Yeah, honey?" she says distractedly, like she expects me to ask her a question about the laundry.

"Is Dad really going to kick David out this time?"

She shrugs. Her eyes are pointed somewhere on the carpet. She takes a sip of her wine, and it leaves a sloppy red stain around her mouth, like a kid slurping Kool-Aid.

"Do something!" I demand. "You can't let this happen. You can't give up." But I know, as soon as it comes out of my mouth, that it isn't true. I know that's exactly what she's done. I know she did it a long time ago.

"Do what, Marcus?" she says, finally managing to look me in the eyes. She's folded over herself, as if she can no longer find the motivation to stay upright. "What can I do?"

"Do something," I say. "Do anything." Anything is better than nothing.

But she shakes her head and takes another sip of wine. She looks at her book and sinks farther into the chair.

here.

IF GOD EXISTS, I'M PRETTY SURE HE'S LAUGHING HIS ASS off right now. He's sitting up there in his cloud recliner with a beer in his hand, elbowing his angel friend and congratulating himself about the epic joke he's playing on me. "What a chump!" they're saying.

It's one hour after being told by my girlfriend's sister that she's in rehab and never wants to see me again, one day after finding out she had a secret life and identity she told me nothing about, and now I'm standing in my living room looking at my mother who I haven't seen in almost two years since she ran off and abandoned us. She's sitting on the couch across from my father, and they're drinking coffee like she's any old guest, as if that is a place where guests sit, as if this is a house that is used to having guests. That must be her car with the Washington plates in the driveway.

"Hi, Marcus," she says, and the sound of her voice sends dull knives through my rib cage.

"What the fuck is going on?" I say.

"Marcus," Dad says. "Why don't you sit down." He is too calm. I don't understand how he can just sit there with the woman who left him and took half his money and destroyed his family.

"No," I say. "This is bullshit. What the hell is she doing here?"

"Marcus," she says, her voice too calm, too controlled. She's sitting so still, so upright. "I know this must be difficult for you. It's understandable that you're upset." She should have fallen into her usual histrionics by now. She should be spewing indecipherable tear-drenched words. This is some weird, restrained version of my mother, with a simple chin-length haircut instead of the long blond I remember. Her face is clean and without makeup. A sweater, jeans, and clogs have replaced the kind of outfits that used to embarrass me, the low-cut blouses and too-tight pants that screamed *Look at me!* How perverse that she finally looks like someone's mother now that she isn't.

"Why are you here?" I growl. "I thought I made it clear that I never wanted to talk to you again when I didn't return any of your calls."

She nods and looks down at her lap. "Yes, of course," she says. "That was absolutely your right. I knew it would take you a long time to forgive me."

"Well, keep waiting. It's never going to happen."

"Marcus, will you please sit down?" Dad says. "Your mother's here because I invited her."

"What?"

"I think it's time for you to let her back into your life."

"How are you the one who gets to decide that? Oh wait, I forgot. You're the boss of everything."

"You sound like a child," he says.

"Why are you on her side? She left you too, you know."

Dad sighs. He should be yelling. Mom should either be curled into herself while he rages, or drunk and raging right back. But they're both so . . . relaxed. This isn't my life. These aren't my parents.

He stands up. "I'm going to leave you two to talk. I'm sure you have a lot of catching up to do." Really, Dad? What a fucking coward. "Do you need anything, Renae?" he says. "More coffee?"

"No, thank you, Bill," she says. "I'm fine."

Who are these people?

"I've been living in Seattle, you know. Where your aunt Katy is?" Mom says after Dad leaves the room to go hide in the kitchen. "Your father and I have been in contact."

"I know."

"I respected the fact that you weren't ready to talk to me, but I still wanted to know what was going on with you. If you weren't going to talk to me, I could at least talk to him."

Like he has any idea, is what I want to say. *Like he even cares.* But I know that would open more floodgates I don't want opened.

"He's worried about you."

"So he calls *you* here to talk to me about it? He's that much of a chicken he has to call his ex-wife to talk to his son?"

"He said he's been trying to talk to you, but you keep pushing him away. He thought I'd have more luck."

"Yeah? What do you think? Do you feel lucky?"

"Can we try this without the sarcasm?"

"I don't know. Can we?" I'm even annoying myself.

"Come on, Marcus. Talk to me. What's going on? Your dad says you're seeing someone. What's she like?"

"No," I say. "We're not going to do this. You can't come walking back into my life after two years and expect to have some heart-to-heart about my girlfriend. We're not going to sit here bonding over a bottle or two or five of wine. We're not friends. I'm not David."

She flinches at the sound of his name. I hurt her and it feels good.

"I know that," she whispers. "Of course I know that."

Silence. Silence so loud my ears burn.

"That's one of the reasons why I've come now," she says. "I know it's just a few days until the anniversary of his death. Your father and I thought this might be an especially difficult time for you." She pauses for a moment, her face contorted in fake sympathy. "Marcus, do you want to talk about David?"

"Fuck no," I say. "Fuck you."

"I'm sorry," she says.

"Your sorry isn't worth shit."

Dad appears in the doorway. "Is everything okay in here?"

"Fine," I say. "I was just leaving." I turn toward the stairway.

"No you don't," he says. "Stay right there."

"It's okay," Mom says with a tired voice. "Let him go. He has every right to be angry."

"Oh, thanks so much for your permission."

I march up the stairs, stomping as hard as I can, but it's not loud enough, not satisfying. The house doesn't shake. Mirrors don't fall from the walls. Lights don't fall from the ceiling and come crashing down on their heads.

I go to my room and turn the music up as loud as I can stand it. I stand in the middle of the room and look around at this place, my cave. No one besides the biweekly cleaning lady has stepped foot in this room since David died. Not until Evie. She was the only one I let in.

I can't do this anymore. This can't be my life.

I water and pick dead leaves off the plants David left when he moved out. Only a dozen remain of the almost thirty plants I started with those three years ago. Even after everything I've done to keep them alive, all the research into indoor gardening, all the watering and rotating and soil fluffing, all the repotting and fertilizers, they still keep on dying.

The plants are watered, and I am alone. Mom's car is gone from the driveway. I call Evie's number, but it's been disconnected. Tomorrow's my last day of junior year, and then summer starts. I should be excited. I should have something to look forward to. I try to think about the future, but there is nothing but empty, useless space. Without Evie. Without David. Without anything or anyone that matters.

I am so sick of this, so sick of myself.

Something has to change.

there.

"WHAT DO YOU THINK?" DAVID SAYS. I CAN'T TELL IF HE IS kidding. There's no way he could really want my opinion about this new shithole apartment he shares with his girlfriend, this life he decided was worth throwing away Yale, worth throwing away our family.

"It's okay," I say.

"Don't get distracted by the way it looks," he says, stamping out his cigarette in the already overflowing ashtray. "That's superficial shit. That's the bullshit people like Dad want you to think is important. Money and power and position. That's their world, Marcus, not ours." He gets up off the ripped and saggy sofa, steps over a pile of clothes on the floor and into the tiny kitchen, and pulls two beers out of the fridge.

"This apartment means freedom," he says, handing me a beer.

This apartment means he's gone. It's final proof of what I've known in my heart for months, as I've been missing my brother even when he's standing right in front of me.

"Did Mom buy you this beer?" I say.

"Yeah." He laughs. "She took me to Trader Joe's and basically told me I could fill up the cart with anything I wanted. I cleared out the frozen pizzas."

What am I supposed to say to that? Congratulations on using Mom's weird codependent need for your devotion to get free groceries?

"It's so funny," David says, lighting another cigarette. "She's the one who always talked about leaving, and I totally beat her to it."

David's girlfriend, Natalie, is lying on the couch next to him, her head resting in his lap. She was already tired after a long night of work at the strip club, then she had a joint and four shots of tequila as soon as she got home, and now she can barely keep her eyes open. "I made really good money tonight," she murmurs. "And I didn't even have to touch anyone." She laughs to herself at the joke I cannot bring myself to understand.

"Don't judge me," she slurs in halfhearted outrage, at an imagined reaction she could not have seen through her closed eyelids.

I am barely more conscious than her. She is snoring now. I cannot open my eyes more than slits. Before I pass out, the last thing I see is David laughing, still completely awake despite having consumed more than twice as much as us. He is stacking things on top of Natalie's prone body, as if she is a table, not a person, as if she is an unfeeling thing—the TV remote, junk mail, a dirty plate.

David's lip is cracked and his eye is swollen and blue. He's been gone for five days and won't tell me where he's been. I called him as soon as I read the letter Mom left in the kitchen, but apparently she had gotten to him first.

I want to talk about her. I want to know what she told him. I want to show him the letter she left for Dad and me, how it explains nothing. It weighs heavy in my pocket, the drunken, scribbled words burning a hole into my leg where they are scrawled across the page:

> *I can't take this anymore. I'm leaving. I'm sorry, Marcus. I love you. Maybe someday I'll figure out how to be a mother, but I am done being a wife.*

I want to know if she told him more than she told me. I want to know how his heart is breaking, if it is in the same shattered pieces as mine.

But he refuses to talk about her. He won't tell me where he's been or how he got the black eye. "She's gone," is all he says. "It's over." He's pacing around the apartment like a trapped animal.

"What's over?" I say. I want to hurt him. I want to hurt somebody. I want to hurt myself. I want to dig into my skin until this pain stops. I need something to make me stop thinking about her, about her absence, about my being left alone in that house with no one on my side.

"Our family," he says. "I'm gone and she's gone."

"I'm still here," I say, but he doesn't hear me.

"Fuck it," he says. He sits down and pulls a small leather bag out of his pocket. I watch as he pulls out a wrinkled piece of burned black tinfoil. A glass pipe. A baggie of brown clumped powder.

Because I don't see any needles, I tell myself David's not a junkie. But, deep down, I know heroin is still heroin, even if you smoke it.

I pull the letter out of my pocket. I shove it in front of him. "Read it," I say. He takes it without looking at me, pulls a lighter out of his pocket, and lights it on fire. I watch the flame climb up the paper and lick his fingers. "David," I say.

His face is empty, blank. No pain, no feeling, nothing. For a split second, I wish I could be as numb as him.

"David!" I pull the letter out of his hand and throw it in the ashtray. It is black, charred, barely solid. The words are gone. It is halfway to ash.

David sits there, looking at his hand with no expression on his face. The tips of his fingers are burned red. They will blister for sure.

"Does it hurt?" I say. I suddenly feel strangely calm. His pain is so big it erases mine.

"No," he says. "Nothing hurts."

I say nothing as I watch him get loaded. I am removed somehow, watching a documentary about a promising kid's life getting destroyed by drugs. It is someone else's brother, someone else's life. He smokes until he can't keep his eyes open. Even after all we've drank together, all the pot we've smoked, the ecstasy, the mushrooms, the acid, he's never been like this. Gone. Barely human. I know in this moment I am going to lose him too.

He sinks into the ratty couch and pulls an unzipped sleeping bag over himself. "I shouldn't have left," he mumbles. "I'm sorry, Marcus."

"You can come back," I say, but he's already sleeping, and I know it isn't true. When he left, there was nothing left for Mom to stay for. Now that she's gone, I know he's never coming home.

David sleeps his junkie sleep, the skin on his face slack, his mouth open and drooling, his mind emptied of its burdens. This deathlike sleep is the only way he knows to find peace. My brother has been replaced by a zombie.

I go home. The house is dark and silent. Dad is out with whatever bimbo he's seeing at the moment. I could trash the place. I could destroy it beyond repair.

But instead, I walk up the grand staircase and down the hall to my bedroom. I don't turn on the lights. I stand in the middle of my room and feel the darkness go on forever, in every direction. No matter what I do or where I go, it will be there. Waiting for me. Following me. I will never get away. Fate is fixed. There are only different shades of darkness.

I grab my left wrist with my right hand. I dig my fingernails into my flesh. The darkness contracts. But my nails are not long enough. I need something sharper to really carve the darkness away.

I am disgusted with myself the moment I think of it, but there is already so much to be disgusted by, what's one more thing? I walk slowly, calmly to the bathroom. I lift my razor from the counter. I remember how proud I was the day I first shaved, how it was David, not Dad, who showed me how.

I pull the plastic away from the blade. The sharp edge reflects the ceiling light as I feel the metal sliver in my hand.

I try not to think. I focus on the steps down the hall. One two three. Back to my room. Back to the darkness of my cave, where I will huddle in the corner, tiny as a mouse, hiding from the beasts that are most hungry, making myself small and bitter tasting so they won't want me.

I lock the door, not that Dad would ever come to this part of the house. I take off my shirt. I turn the lights off and light one candle. Everything else stops existing. My world is the dull circle illuminated by that weak flame. Reality flickers in and out.

This blade, this tiny, sharp thing. It has the power to shrink the world to the size of a narrow line. A centimeter, an inch. A moment of nothing. Just a finite location, so small there is no room for David, no room for Mom or Dad or anyone else whose absence demands so much space inside me. I press down and meet resistance. I press down, harder, and in a split second my pain funnels to this minuscule opening, this dot of light.

I cut myself to let them go. I open my skin to release them. I slice them away. I bleed them out. The pain makes me clean. And the blood speaks louder than I ever could. The blood is my voice. It tells me I'm alive.

here.

I'M NOT SURE WHY I EVEN CAME TO SCHOOL TODAY. IT'S the last day of junior year, but I have nothing to celebrate. All my papers have been turned in, all my tests taken. Everybody else is making a big deal about cleaning out their lockers, saying goodbye to teachers in a final ass-kissing attempt to ensure good letters of recommendation, comparing summer travel plans or impressive internships, but we all know the real purpose of today is to confer about what parties are happening and what girls will be there and who has what drugs. Maybe this isn't how it is for some students, but I don't know those people.

I'm sitting where I usually sit at lunch, at the table in the corner with the school stoners. Funny how we have this title when practically half the school smokes as much or more than us. And many of them do even harder stuff. Cocaine is especially popular among the school elite. Some of the top guys here, the ones with the most important parents, the ones destined for the Ivy League, are full-blown cokeheads, snorting lines in the bathroom between classes. That and popping Adderall, which is the same thing as speed, which is basically the same thing as meth, but these guys wouldn't be caught dead saying they do such a low-class drug as that. They can convince themselves that a prescription isn't as serious as a street drug, even though it's just as addictive and just as deadly. And they keep getting away with it, keep getting bailed out of whatever trouble they get in because the system is designed to not let them fail. I'm sure some black kid in an Oakland public school would have an entirely different consequence if he got caught doing the shit some of these guys do. I've never been quite sure where I fall on that spectrum, but I certainly don't want to find out.

The guys at my table are a hodgepodge of people who don't quite fit in. We got the stoner label because we don't spend as much time keeping up appearances as the rest of the school. But I wouldn't say we're friends. My out-of-school contact with these guys is minimal. We stand next to each other at parties, I guess. But I don't go to movies with them or hang out at their houses or whatever it is friends do. Some of them do that but not me. David was always the source of my social life. When he died, my social life died with him.

"Are you going to Tyson's party tonight?" someone says, and it takes me a few seconds to realize the question's directed at me.

"Huh? Oh. No, I don't think so." Then for some reason I add, "I have plans with my girlfriend." The lie makes me feel lonelier.

"Why don't you bring her?" someone else says.

"And subject her to you assholes? No way." Ha-ha-ha. Everyone laughs. I learned a long time ago that sarcasm is the best way to keep my distance from people.

I feel a hand on my shoulder. I look around to see Gabe, my dealer. One of the richest kids in here, I have no idea why he has the need to sell drugs. He definitely doesn't need the money. Maybe it's about the power. Maybe it's the only way he's found that makes him feel important.

"Hey, Marcus," he says.

"Hey."

"Need anything? I got it all right now."

I think about it for a moment, and a realization pops in my head like a bubble, my answer so surprisingly clear. "No," I say. Even though I have been out of pot for a couple of days, even though normally I would have searched him out by now, fiending to buy more. "I'm good," I say.

"You sure?"

"Yeah, man."

He shrugs and moves on to the guy sitting next to me, who already has his money out.

No, I don't want to buy any weed today. I don't want to get high. I don't want my head in the clouds when there's so much down here that needs my attention.

Something needs to change, and maybe that something is me. Maybe I need to start doing everything differently. Maybe I will take that internship at my dad's office and start reading those college brochures. Maybe I'll start eating more vegetables. If I clean up my act, maybe Evie will want to be with me again. She'll get out of rehab and I'll be waiting for her, changed, better. I will prove I'm good enough for her. She'll give me another chance. We'll start over, without lies, without secrets, without drugs to keep us hidden.

My phone buzzes in my pocket with a text message.

Marcus, this is your mother, it reads, from a number I don't recognize. *I'm sorry about the way things went last night. Can I take you out for coffee after school? Just this one time, then you never have to see me again if you don't want to.*

What the hell.

Sure, I text back.

If I'm going to change, I might as well go all the way.

there.

AFTER MOM LEAVES, I TAKE OVER HER JOB OF CHECKING on David. I bring him meals, I do his laundry, I clean his bathroom and pay his unopened bills, and watch him fade away. No matter what I do, no matter how I help, David's world gets smaller and smaller until it's only the size of his sunken seat on the sofa and as far as his arms can reach to the ashtray, to his bag of poison.

"Natalie and I haven't fucked in weeks," he says as I open the kitchen window to air the place out. The stack of dirty dishes in the sink is growing mold. Even if she let him touch her, I'm not sure David's body is capable of that anymore. He has a hard time making it to the corner market to buy cigarettes. David had always been big and muscular like Dad, but now he is skinnier than me, and he seems to have lost several inches of height, if that's possible.

"I'm pretty sure she's dating a chick from work. I can't remember the last time she came home."

Home. Is that what he calls this hellhole?

"Fine with me," he says, his eyelids drooping. "All she ever did was . . ." His voice trails off. His thought stops midsentence as sleep takes over.

"Hey," I say, shoving his shoulder. "Wake up."

"Why?" he mumbles from wherever he is, and I cannot come up with a good answer.

Today, my job is to figure out what's wrong with his heater. It's the middle of the summer, but David is always cold. Every day, it's something new—he needs me to loan him twenty bucks, he needs me to bring him a gallon of milk, he needs this favor or that favor, countless things that normal people know how to do themselves. And I keep doing them because I don't want to know what will happen if I say no.

Sometimes I talk to David when he's passed out. I wait until he's totally gone, when shaking him doesn't make him blink, after his head has fallen back and his mouth hangs open, and his upper body slides down the back of the couch until he's half lying, half sitting, his body contorted at a strange angle. Occasionally, he mutters something that almost sounds like words, but I know he's not with me. I pretend the silence means he's listening. I pretend I am not the loneliest person in the world.

I wonder what all the girls who used to chase him would think of him now, in clothes that haven't been washed in weeks, with his hair all grown out and matted like a Brillo pad. The guy who should have been valedictorian, the guy who got accepted early decision to Yale, the guy with perfect teeth and six-pack abs who could get any girl he wanted in all the Bay Area—he's now on his way to joining the ranks of that homeless guy who hangs out on Telegraph selling sculptures he makes out of tinfoil, with the one giant dreadlock as thick as a tree branch, with sticks and leaves poking out of it. David and I used to joke about it being a nest for rats, imagining all the different vermin that could live inside it.

David scratches his head in his sleep, and his whole scalp moves. I suddenly feel itchy. I try not to think about what kind of things could be living in this furniture.

There are really only a few things that separate David from that homeless guy on Telegraph—his education, who our father is, the fact that he was at one time handsome and charming enough to get a girl with her own apartment to like him enough to let him live with her. But all that has faded by this point. David's genius is irrelevant; he is so strung out, his brain cannot form coherent thoughts anymore. Mom is gone and Dad has disowned him. I know Natalie is going to stop accepting my money for his share of the rent soon and finally kick him out. After that, I don't know what's going to keep him from living on the streets, what's going to keep him from selling garbage on the sidewalk. What will he have after he finally loses everything? Me? What good am I if I'm all he has left?

I leave him on the couch to use the bathroom. To say it is filthy would be an understatement. It smells like piss and mildew. The counter of the sink is caked with dirt and hair and soap scum. Black mold surrounds the window. The toilet bowl has a black ring inside, like it hasn't been washed in years. My shoes stick to the floor. There is no soap to wash my hands, so I rinse them under warm water and wipe them on my pants. No way am I going to touch those towels.

When I open the door into the living room, David's bent over the chair where I had been sitting, going through the pockets of my jacket. He takes out my wallet and opens it, pulling out most of the cash and a Starbucks gift card. I say nothing. He puts the wallet back in my pocket, lies back down on the couch, and closes his eyes. I wait a few more moments before entering the room, so he won't know I saw him.

"I'm going to head out," I say.

"All right." David opens his eyes and reaches for his pack of cigarettes on the coffee table. "See you later, little brother." Like nothing. Like he doesn't know what he did.

I know suddenly there is no coming back from this. I know David is lost for good. Whatever I thought I've been doing— waiting for him to get better, to snap out of it, to come back to me—that is never going to happen. He's lying in his deathbed, and I'm his loyal attendant, holding his hand while he dies.

David doesn't even take the Narcotics Anonymous pamphlets I brought for him. He turns his head back to the television and leaves me standing here with my arm outstretched. I haven't seen him move from the couch in days. If he eats or goes to the bathroom, it's before I arrive or after I leave. He certainly hasn't taken a shower recently. The apartment smells like someone getting ready to die.

"Come on," I say, throwing the pamphlets on the filthy coffee table. "Won't you at least read them?"

"Nope," he says, switching the channel from one daytime talk show to another.

"I'm trying to help you."

"That's very nice of you, Marcus, but no help needed. Thank you. Have a nice day. Will you look at this shit?"

The TV is turned to a show about eating disorders. A girl my age sits on a stage with her crying mother. She can't weigh more than eighty pounds.

"People are so fucking crazy," David says, with absolutely no irony.

"Will you at least take a shower?"

"Jesus, Marcus," David says, finally looking at me. "Get a fucking life and stop trying to control mine. You're getting to be as bad as Dad."

"I care about you," I say. "I'm worried about you."

He looks me in the eyes, his lips curled into a sneer, exposing brown, rotted teeth. He reminds me more of a dog than my brother. A stray. Something feral. A fighting dog.

"Marcus, you're fucking pathetic," he says, and my blood drains out of my head and arms and legs, into my chest, where it weighs dark and heavy.

"David—" I begin, but he cuts me off.

"You've been following me around your whole life," he says. "Why can't you leave me alone?"

"I'm trying to help. I—"

"I don't need your fucking help! How many times do I have to say it before it gets through your stupid head? I don't need you. I don't want you here."

"David—"

"Leave."

"I just—"

"Fucking leave, Marcus!"

I turn around before he can see the tears stinging my eyes. I walk out before he can say anything else. I leave, like he told me to. Just like everyone else.

I keep expecting to look at my phone and see a text from David asking to borrow money, to bring over some toilet paper, to buy him a burger. But days go by with nothing. Then weeks. I do everything I can think of, smoke everything I have, so I won't think about him festering in that apartment. But nothing eliminates my worry. I know I'm losing him. My brother, my one and only friend.

I keep texting. I keep calling. I say I want to see him. I say I'm sorry, but I'm not even sure what I'm apologizing for. I am too happy to receive his sporadic short, cryptic texts back. I am grateful for his lies about being busy. At least I know he's alive.

Something is my fault, I know it. I failed him. My guilt fuses with fear and love, and it's getting harder and harder to tell the three apart.

So when David finally texts asking me to let him come over one night when Dad is working late in the city, I say yes. He tells me he wants to grab a few things from his old room, but I know what he's really there to do.

I sit in the kitchen while he roots around upstairs. After twenty minutes or so, he comes back down, his backpack bulging with things he's not supposed to have. I tell myself he took things like Dad's cuff links and watches, some electronics, harmless things made out of money. I don't think about other possibilities. I pretend I don't know what else Dad has. I pretend I don't notice the feeling in the pit of my stomach that tonight has set in motion something I will never be able to stop.

I drive him back to his apartment without mentioning any of the things that are spinning around in my head, nothing about the loneliness that threatens to swallow me up every night when I'm home alone in my room, nothing about the box where I keep my drugs and razor blades, nothing about the net of scars that's growing on my shoulder, nothing about the infinite layers of pain that I can't get to the bottom of no matter how deep I cut. The person I want to talk to isn't there, hasn't been there for a long time. He's a skeleton with skin, inflated with smoke.

here.

I MEET MOM AT A COFFEE SHOP ON FOURTH STREET IN Berkeley, which is a very different scene from the places I usually hang out. This place is populated mostly by rich moms from the hills, surrounded by shopping bags from upscale boutiques as they sip their soy chais. Mom used to do a lot of damage on this street, when shopping and drinking were her only hobbies. I wonder if she's gained any other hobbies in the two years since she left.

"What are you going to get?" she asks me, trying too hard to appear relaxed and chipper. The side of her mouth twitches.

I look at the menu, drawn in careful calligraphy on the wall behind the counter. Maybe the new me should try to eat something besides the usual burritos and snacks and pastries I live on. There's something called a Green Power Smoothie that costs nine dollars. Mom's paying, so I get that.

We sit at a table by the window. Mom holds her coffee cup with both hands, as if she's freezing and trying to warm up.

I take a sip of the smoothie and nearly gag. It tastes like grass and seaweed.

"This is disgusting," I say. "I'm going to get a chocolate croissant."

Mom pulls bills out of her wallet and shoves them at me. "Is this enough? I have more if you need it. Get anything you want."

I take the money. I want to tell her to stop trying so hard. No amount of money is going to make me forgive her.

When I get back, Mom is deep in thought. "So?" I say with my mouth full of croissant, savoring the more familiar flavors of butter and sugar.

"I'm so happy you changed your mind and agreed to talk to me," she says. She is looking down at her coffee. Her fingers cross and uncross.

"Everyone deserves a second chance, right?" Did that really come out of my mouth?

Mom looks up at me, her eyes wet with the beginning of tears, and I feel a dull surge of anger. She has no right to be sad. She's the one who fucked up. If anyone should be sad, it's me.

"God, I can't start crying already," she says, wiping her eyes. "I haven't even started yet. My sponsor thinks it's too soon, but I need to do this." She takes a deep breath, and I prepare myself for whatever's about to come. "There's a lot I need to tell you," she begins. "To make amends. I don't expect you to ever forgive me for leaving. But I want you to understand. Regardless of how you feel about me, I hope at least you won't have this weighing on your heart."

"Did you rehearse this?" I say.

She laughs. "Yeah. Like a million times."

"I can tell."

"That bad?"

I shrug. Honestly, I'd say the fact that I'm still sitting here listening to her means she's doing pretty well. But I'm not going to tell her that.

"First of all," she continues, "I need you to know that I never wanted to leave you, Marcus. I was leaving your father. I was leaving a version of myself that I hated."

"But I was collateral damage?" I say. The old, dull anger weighing in my chest turns a little sharper.

"I guess you could say that."

"What about David? Were you leaving him?" It seems so strange saying his name out loud in front of her—illicit, forbidden—as if naming him will unleash some sort of dark magic.

She looks away, takes a sip of her coffee. "In some ways, yes," she finally says, her voice surprisingly strong. "I guess you could say that. Our relationship wasn't healthy."

"You don't have to tell me that."

"I was suffocating. I was extremely depressed, suicidal even, and I was very much an alcoholic. *Am* an alcoholic. I've been sober nine months now, but it's a disease I will always have. That's part of why I'm here, making these amends. It's part of my recovery."

"How nice for you."

She flinches. "I'm trying to make things right. I'll do anything to make things right."

"So you think taking me out for coffee and apologizing is going to make things right?" I can feel my anger boiling, rising in my throat. Cruel words burn in my mouth.

"Of course not. But it's a start. It's the first step in healing."

"Step, huh? Is that an AA thing? So what's the next step?"

I wait for her answer while she takes another deep breath. "I'm thinking of moving back," she says. "I want to go back to school to get my master's in social work."

"You can't do that in Seattle?"

"I was hoping I could be part of your life again. In this year before you go off to college."

I taste the bitter green of the smoothie in my throat. "Maybe it's too late for that." My voice is acid, sharp, burning.

I can tell she's using all her strength to not cry, to not make a scene. Such a change from the mother I remember, whose feelings were always so careless and out of control, bursting out of her and making a mess with no regard for who would have to step in it. She nods and looks me in the eyes and for a moment I see the woman before that, the one from my childhood, the mother who took us on adventures, the person I thought had to be the most beautiful woman in the world.

"But maybe it's not," she says. "Maybe it's not too late."

I don't know what I'm feeling, if there's a name for this mix of resentment and nostalgia and hope, for this glimmer of love breaking through my tornado of anger and confusion.

No. A few words at a coffee shop cannot undo years of damage. A half-assed apology cannot make up for the fact that she left me, left David when he needed her most. She hasn't explained anything. She is nowhere near off the hook.

"Why did you leave?" I say.

"I told you," she says. "I was miserable."

"That's not enough. A lot of moms are miserable, but they don't leave."

"I know."

"It's, like, against nature or something. Dads leave, not moms."

"I know."

"How does a mother leave her own kids?" My voice breaks, whether in sadness or anger, I can't tell. But my throat feels like it's going to close up.

"I don't know." She is shrunken, gone. "I don't know how I did it." She is a shell.

"If you're going to do something like that, you have to have a reason."

"I couldn't love anymore." Now the tears are coming. Now her voice is thick with them.

"You couldn't love us?"

"I couldn't love anyone."

"You loved David."

She makes a sound like a whimper, then says, "David used up my love until there wasn't any left."

"You blame him now? I thought you blamed Dad."

She shakes her head. "I couldn't save David. That's the only thing I knew I had to do, and I couldn't do it."

"There were plenty of other things you had to do, Mom.

David wasn't the only one who needed you."

She nods. She swallows. "I was dead, Marcus. I wanted to die."

"Yeah," I say. "I guess it runs in the family." I have never wanted to hurt anyone more in my life.

"Marcus, you have no idea how hard it was for me. How hard it's been living with that guilt and shame. I can't sleep at night." She is weeping now. Finally, she is making a scene. She is making this all about her.

There she is. There's the mother I know.

"You have no idea how much I missed you both. I knew it was all my fault, and that hurt so much. This last year has been so hard. You have no idea—"

"Okay, you can stop now," I say. "I don't need to hear any more."

"Oh, Marcus," she weeps. "I know there's no excuse for what I did, but I want to make it up to you. I'll do anything."

People look at us with annoyance more than concern. How dare we disturb their right to an expensive coffee break? Who is this black boy making this pretty white lady cry?

"Mom, stop crying. You're making a scene. You're embarrassing yourself. This is pathetic."

She stops crying. She sniffles. She looks up at me with a sudden clarity in her eyes. She says, "You sound just like your father."

That's when I storm out and leave.

"Marcus, wait!" she calls, but I don't even turn around.

She made a choice and she's going to have to live with it. Family isn't just something you have on reserve, ready to be in your life when you're ready for it. She can't leave, then decide she wants a kid again as soon as it becomes convenient. Maybe she's lonely, maybe she thinks she's figured herself out, maybe she thinks she's ready to be a mother again, as if nine months sober is enough to change everything about who she is.

I am done. My heart is so full of pain and betrayal, there is no room for forgiveness. I have already accepted that I do not have a mother, and I am not going back. I sure as hell am not going to risk getting hurt again while she tests some desperate new theory that maybe, just maybe, she can try to love me as much as she loved David.

there.

PEOPLE COME TO DAVID'S FUNERAL WHO NEVER MET HIM—
Dad's colleagues, people who want to be Dad's colleagues. It is a
networking event, and he is the perfect politician. He never breaks
character, neither smiles nor cries. He accepts the long line of con-
dolences with serious grace. He is a man beyond suffering.

I mostly sleep through the service. A priest I've never even
met describes a made-up version of my brother, someone I don't
know, someone who had become a stranger, someone I hadn't
seen for a long time. The David he talks about, the one everyone
wants to remember and the only one we're acknowledging today,
is the David that was long gone, way before he died, the one I have
already gotten used to missing.

I wake to an organ blaring weird syrupy music, just in time to
follow my dad out of the chapel and into the lobby. I am stoned
out of my mind and barely able to stand beside him as people take
turns shaking our hands. I am glad for the hugs because in those

small moments, I can rely on someone else to keep me upright.

I say "thank you" more times than I can count. Nodding my head takes on its own kind of surreal rhythm. I am finding a kind of peace in the waves of sympathy, but then there's a rustle in the fabric of the day, some kind of disturbance in the corner of my view, voices raised, people moving, an added electricity in the air.

"Jesus Christ," I hear Dad say under his breath. "Fucking hell."

And then I see her. Mom. Weaving through the crowd of people, her sister Katy following behind her with arms outstretched, as if she is trying to catch a wandering child. "Renae," I hear Aunt Katy scold above the din of whispers announcing Mom's arrival. "This wasn't a good idea. We should go."

"I'm not going," Mom slurs. "This is my son's funeral. I have a right to go to my son's funeral."

"Renae, honey," Mrs. Alsace says, our neighbor from down the street. "The funeral is over. It already happened." She is speaking gently, in low tones, trying to preserve some kind of dignity for my mom.

"No," Mom says, then nearly trips on a bench against the wall. "Who put that there?"

"Renae," Dad says in his lowest register. He strides over to where she is standing. The crowd has made a circle of space around her, as if getting too close will contaminate them somehow. My aunt has her hand on Mom's arm, steadying her.

"I'm so sorry, Bill," Aunt Katy says. "She insisted on coming. I thought it would be good for her. We flew down from Seattle early this morning." Katy looks at my mom, at her disheveled hair and wrinkled blouse, at her empty gaze at her feet. "She had a few drinks on the plane," she says softly, but there's no use trying to be discreet. Everyone is silent, still, listening.

Mom's not moving. She won't look up from her feet. I can see the shame in her slumped-over shoulders, in the growing-out roots of her hair, in her purse strap sliding halfway down her arm. Shame radiates from her skin like mist.

"Renae, it's time for you to leave," Dad says. "Our lawyers will be in touch. There's nothing we need to talk about here."

"I want to see my son," Mom says, her voice as quiet as breath.

"Your son is dead," Dad says, and that's when I finally leave. I make my way through the crowd and out of the building before I have a chance to find out which son she was talking about.

The church is only a few blocks from my house, so I walk home. The caterers are setting up for the reception, placing beautifully constructed platters of expensive hors d'oeuvres throughout the cold living room. There is nothing here that says death. There's nothing that says David. This could be a wedding reception or an anniversary party. A bunch of people who didn't even know David will mingle with glasses of wine. There are only two people who really loved David, and neither of us will be here.

I go up to my room. I don't care if Dad comes up and catches me, if I get in trouble for skipping the reception. I take out the box I used to keep my treasures in, all the stupid little keepsakes from my childhood that I thought held some kind of power. Those are all long gone. All that's left are my drugs and the tools I use to cut my pain into my skin. I look at the shiny, sharp objects lying there like miniature surgical instruments. What a stupid irony that they resemble such things, so useful, meant to preserve life, while I defile it again and again, turning my body into a torture chamber, punishing myself for hurting by making myself hurt more.

David is gone. My brother is dead.

This is my good-bye, one final torture. I take the X-Acto knife out of my box and pull up the leg of my pants. I start cutting. I feel the immediate rush of adrenaline as the blood starts to trickle. I don't know which is warmer—blood or tears. But they are both here, both soaking me to my core.

The blade cuts through me, deeper than skin, deeper than muscle and bone.

I carve his initials: *DL*. I carve the date of his death. I crack open the ink tube of a ballpoint pen and let the black liquid mix with my blood.

I started this bullshit when my mother left. I am ending it with David.

It is over. I am done with pain. I am done with love.

Now into the garbage with everything—these razor blades and needles, this X-Acto knife and tiny scissors. I whisper my vow into the darkness: I will never cut again. I will not trade one pain for another. I will not open myself up for any kind of torture, be it blades or trust or heartbreak. This will be one final scar to end them all, a final hardening of skin. A final shell. A final shield.

I tie a bandanna around my open wound. The best I can hope for is to not make too much of a mess.

Now this is what's left in the box that used to hold my dreams:

a bag full of weed and the stained glass pipe David bought me for my fourteenth birthday.

This is enough. This is all I need now.

My only choice is to smoke until I can't keep my eyes open, to smoke until I know I will sleep without dreaming, to smoke until I erase the entire day, the entire year, my entire life.

Knocks on the door. One two three. "Marcus," Dad's voice says. I can't remember the last time he was up here, in my part of the house. "Marcus, are you all right?" I am dizzy. I am almost gone. His voice sounds like it is miles away. Part of me wants to go to it. Part of me wants to speak, to tell him to open the door and come in, to find me here half-conscious, to pull me up and shake me awake. But my voice is gone. The door stays closed. He says nothing more. He leaves me in my cave and returns to the party.

you.

THERE WAS MAGIC, EVIE. YOU HAVE TO REMEMBER. THOSE moments we forgot to be scared. Those moments we trusted each other so completely we ceased being bodies, when we were so free we turned into light, when we could not tell the difference between our skin and air and earth and water, when we were so big we became everything.

The water held us and made me brave. I had decided you were the one I wanted to show everything—my scars, the ones I always hid. They are the scars that tell the story of my mom leaving and of David dying. They are the physical proof of a pain so huge I could not keep it inside my body.

But then the air shifted. It always shifted. I'd catch a glimpse of you and it would light up the sky, but then the clouds would come and you'd get that look on your face that became so familiar, the look that told me you were gone, I had lost you, and I would have to wait until the next time you were truly present. I grasped at those rare, small moments when your eyes met mine and I knew you were with me, your mind not wandering, not getting lost in the past or the future or somewhere else you'd rather be. I knew I'd have to get used to waiting and become satisfied with those snippets of breath and skin, those fragments of intoxicating *now*.

And then the light would fade. The magic would be over, only partly revealed. That's the story of us. Over and over. Light and darkness and light again. And right now, the darkness is winning.

here.

MY DREADLOCKS LOOK LIKE DEAD BLACK CATERPILLARS on the bathroom floor. The clippers buzz as I shave my scalp, which tingles with the sudden absence of weight. I imagine my hair follicles all taking a deep breath.

Today is the anniversary of David's death.

Today will not be about him.

I've been sober for six days, a new record. It's been almost a year since the last time I cut. I've finally started looking through the college brochures that have been collecting dust ever since they arrived in the mail. I've decided to take the internship at my dad's office at the courthouse in San Francisco, which starts tomorrow.

I look at myself in the mirror. My head seems too small now, misshapen. I feel slightly off balance. I'm wearing my school uniform—a black suit and white shirt. I decided against the tie. That would be overkill. Maybe this is all overkill. But I want to look respectable, trustworthy. I want to look like a nice guy. Because I'm about to do the dumbest thing so far in my quest for Evie, way worse than stalking Jenica at school.

I sit in my car for a while before working up enough nerve to get out and go ahead with my crazy plan. As I walk up to the front door of Evie's house, it strikes me how strange it is that I've never actually done this before—never picked her up at home, never walked her back after a date, never been inside her house. These are more signs that something was off, signs I should have seen long ago but chose not to.

The sound of my fist on the wooden door is jarring in the peaceful evening. It's the time of night when everyone is home from work and kids are playing in backyards before dinner. And I am going to disrupt all that.

The door opens, my heart stops for a moment, and I know how it is possible for people to die of fright.

"Can I help you?" a man who must be Evie's dad says suspiciously. He looks like a typical Berkeley dad—medium height, medium build, brown hair, glasses, with the air of someone with a postgraduate education. He wasn't at the hospital when I brought Evie in. He has no idea who I am. I probably look like a Jehovah's Witness to him, all clean-cut and wearing a suit.

I open my mouth to begin the speech I've been rehearsing all day, but before I have a chance to speak, Jenica comes swooping in, wedging herself in front of her father, trying to pull the door closed behind her. "This is a classmate from school, Dad," she says. "He just came to talk to me about the comments we got on a final project. I'll talk to him outside."

"Uh, okay," he says, obviously confused. "He can come inside, you know. Don't you want to offer him something to drink?"

Jenica catches my eye, and I can feel the heat of her fury. I can almost hear her psychically yelling at me, *Get the hell out of here NOW!*

I didn't come this far to talk to Jenica on the front lawn.

"Mr. Whinsett?" I say as Jenica manages to scoot him out of the way and start to shut the door behind her. He catches the door with his hand before it closes.

"Yes?" he says, his face suddenly serious.

"Don't," Jenica pleads.

"My name is Marcus Lyon," I begin. "I am in love with your daughter Evie. We have been dating for quite a while. I have been trying to get in contact with her. I need to know if she's okay."

In the wake of my words, there is silence. Then the sound of dishes coming from what must be the kitchen, a murmur of voices.

Evie. I step forward without thinking. Then I feel the strong hands of a furious father on my chest, shoving me back.

"Get the hell out of my house," he says.

"Marcus, just leave," Jenica cries. "Please."

"I know that you want to protect her," I say quickly, knowing I don't have much time before he slams the door in my face. "But you don't understand. I care about Evie. I want her to be healthy, too. I'm not bad. I'm not going to hurt her." This is coming out all wrong. This is not what I wanted to say.

"Don't you think it's a little too late for that?" Evie's dad says, stepping toward me, his voice shaking with anger. If I stay here any longer, I'm going to get hurt.

"What's going on out there?"

Evie's voice. From the kitchen.

Evie's face. Her body. Emerging from the doorway.

My heart stops. It bursts. It flies out of my chest and goes to her.

"Evie," I say.

She freezes. Her face goes white. She takes a shallow breath and holds it. She doesn't breathe as she meets my eyes, as they speak unfathomable shock and fear and sadness.

"Get out of here!" Evie's dad bellows. "Jenica, get me the phone. I'm going to call the cops." Jenica is crying too hard to move.

"Wait," I say. "Evie, tell them. Tell them it's not my fault."

She is stone. She is ice. She has not moved a millimeter since she saw me.

Evie's mom enters from the kitchen, looks around at the still tableau, then registers my presence at the front door. "What is *he* doing here?"

"Pam, call the cops," Evie's dad says. I hear his words. Evie's mom picks up the phone in the living room and starts dialing, and I know I should be scared, but all that matters is Evie's eyes still locked on mine.

"Just leave, Marcus," Jenica begs.

"Evie," I say as Jenica grabs my arm. "Tell them. Please! Tell them the truth."

She looks away. She says nothing. Jenica shuts the door in front of my face. I hear the deadbolt lock. Then silence.

I can't drive. I can barely see. Anger and hurt cloud my eyes, fill my ears with static. I want to tear into my skin until I reach muscle, until I reach bone. But I can't—not here, not now. So I run. It is the only thing I can think of. Moving my body is the only thing I can do to keep my mind and heart from ripping me apart from the inside.

I tear off my jacket and run down the tree-lined street. I have no idea where I'm going or what I'm doing. I need to get out of here, out of myself. But I have no drugs to do it, and even if I did, I know they wouldn't solve anything. Maybe if I run far enough I will find the end of the world and fall off.

Whoop, whoop. The sky is sliced open with the sudden scream of sirens. Not in the distance, not the usual long monotonous dirge, but right here, right behind me, two short yelps so close they ring inside my head. Cars all around me reflect flashing red lights.

"Young man," says a muddled, amplified voice. "Stop running right now."

I turn around and the car is just feet behind me. The red lights spin quietly as the car stops in the middle of the street and two cops get out.

"Stay right there," says one of them, a young black cop. His hand is on his gun. "Don't move."

"What's going on?" I say, and my voice sounds distant, like I'm hearing it through a long tube. The world is suddenly tiny. Everything is in slow motion. The air throbs with the spinning red lights. My heart bursts through my ribs.

"Can you tell us what you're doing in this neighborhood?" the other cop says.

"I was visiting a friend."

"Why were you running?" the black one says. They are standing too close to me. They are closing in. I can't breathe. I can't speak.

"We got a call about someone matching your description bothering a family up the street," says the black one. "Do you know anything about that?"

"I was visiting a friend," I repeat. I can hear a tinge of hostility enter my voice. "If her parents want to call it 'bothering,' that's their problem."

What am I doing? The first thing a man with dark skin knows is to never, ever talk back to a cop.

"What's with the attitude?" the black cop says.

"I didn't do anything wrong." Anger takes over my fear, like a delicious poison spreading through my body. There is nothing I can do to stop it.

"People don't usually run when they didn't do anything wrong."

He's too close. I can smell mustard and meat on his breath. Some kind of metal band winds around my chest, tighter and tighter, faster and faster, until it's red-hot, until it bursts and incinerates everything containing my rage.

"Fuck. You." I say it slowly, deeply, looking straight into the black cop's beady, power-drunk eyes.

The world spins. It is a tornado of hands and arms and metal. My shoulder tweaks as he pulls my arms back. My wrists burn inside the too-tight handcuffs.

"What the fuck are you doing?" I yell. "You can't do this. I didn't do anything wrong."

"Looks like you're coming with us," the white cop says with a sigh, like he's bored, like this is a usual day at the office.

I stumble as the black cop pushes me toward the car. His hand is on the top of my head, guiding me into the back. I go limp as soon as I touch the hard plastic seat. I stop fighting. This is happening. This is really happening. There's nothing I can say or do to stop it. It doesn't matter what the truth is.

I look out the window at the few people on the sidewalk who have stopped to watch. A tiny Chihuahua on a pink studded leash barks hysterically. Curious faces stare out of windows. A black boy, no older than five, watches the scene from inside his house, his tiny arm wrapped tight around a teddy bear. The inside of the car smells like puke and toxic cleanser.

Both cops get in and we start driving. One of them says something into the police radio, but I can't understand it. My brain seems strangely incapable of processing information. I am in a cop car. I am in handcuffs. But I have no idea what it means.

"Am I being arrested?" I hear my voice say. But they are talking about baseball. The thick plastic barrier between us is a desert hundreds of miles thick.

"What are the charges?" I say. One of them is an A's fan, and the other likes the Giants.

I close my eyes. I imagine a pain worse than this.

"Your dad's here," says the female cop at the front desk of the police station. She doesn't look up at me. I'm not worth even that.

I've been sitting on this bench for two hours, replaying the few minutes of events that got me here, over and over in my head. With each repeat, my shame deepens. I keep seeing Evie's face. I keep hearing her silence.

Dad walks in with the white cop who picked me up. They're talking in low tones and I can't hear what they're saying. He's nodding; his mouth is a thin, serious line.

"Let's go," Dad says, grabbing my arm, much tighter than necessary. "You're not being charged with anything."

I stand up. I wait for more. But he says nothing. I can't read his face.

"I didn't do anything illegal, Dad."

"Let's go, Marcus," he says again, not meeting my eyes.

"Can't you talk to someone?" I say, even though I know I shouldn't. But someone needs to suffer for this injustice. Someone besides me. "Can't you get those cops in trouble or something? They were abusing their power. It was racial profiling."

"God dammit, Marcus," Dad snarls. He grabs my arm even harder and pulls me out the door.

It's halfway to night when we get outside. I wonder what Evie's doing right now. I wonder what she told her parents.

"Why didn't you say anything?" I say.

"Let it go," he says, walking ahead, so quiet I can barely hear him.

"Let it go?" I say. "They're the ones who broke the law. You have to do something."

He stops walking and turns around. We are standing on the front steps of the Berkeley police department. The sky burns the dark orange of sunset.

"Marcus, listen to me. You were a young black man running down the middle of the street of a nice neighborhood in Berkeley. A nice white man called the cops because he said you were bothering his nice white teenage daughter. It doesn't matter what you say. It doesn't matter what the truth is."

"But you're a *judge*, Dad," I say. "You're like their *boss*."

"I could be president of the United States and I'd still be a nigger to most people in the country," he says.

I breathe. I swallow. I feel sick. I want to claw at my skin until I tear it off, until I'm raw.

Dad shakes his head. "What is this even about? A girl? All this over a girl?"

I start walking. I am not going to talk to him about this. I am not going to talk to him about anything. "I should go get my car."

"Give me the address and Monica and I will go pick it up."

"I can do it."

"Marcus, I don't want you going anywhere near that house."

"Fine."

I follow him to his pimped-out Mercedes. I get inside, sink

into the plush leather seat, listen to the jazz on his top-of-the-line stereo. Is he saying that none of his money, none of his power and accomplishments, gives him the right to stand up for his son against some cops who abused their power? Or is this an excuse? Is the truth that he didn't even want to?

"What are you doing, Marcus?" he says as he pulls out of the parking space. "Are you trying to turn out like your brother?"

"I can't believe you just said that."

He doesn't respond. His teeth gnash. I know what his anger looks like. I've been watching it my whole life. But this is something different, something more. Something worse.

I want to break something. I want to break everything.

there.

David's eyes, clouded over with smoke. A different smoke from the one I know, not herby and benign. This one is too sweet. Poisoned candy.

there.

My mother's body draped over the too-large armchair. "Mom, wake up." I shake her. Nothing.

you.

Your tears were so loud, they drowned everything out. My thoughts, my feelings—just whispers compared to your screams.

there.

Tinfoil everywhere, tiny blackened crumpled silver. Junkie confetti.

there.

Blinds pulled. The house dark. Black, except for the tiny red ember of my mother's cigarette. I hear her inhale and the red glows, illuminates her face.

"You're not supposed to smoke in here," I say.

She says nothing.

you.

Evie, you were right in front of me, but I couldn't find you.

there.

She puts the cigarette out on the arm of the chair. The living room smells like burning leather. "Are you happy now?" she slurs, and I have to find my way up the stairs in the dark.

you.

I thought if I loved you enough, if I came running every time you called, maybe that would save you. If I said yes every time you asked for anything. If I never said no.

there.

His tooth is brown and rotting. I can smell it. I try to convince him to go to the dentist, I am sure Dad will pay for it, but David refuses. "I don't need his dirty money," he says as he snorts a pile of brown powder with a rolled-up dollar bill.

there.

Mom, don't you know you're killing him?

here.

Razor blade edge. Red blossoms turn into a stream. There is nothing but this blood, nothing but this clear, simple pain. Unambiguous. Perfect. Comforting. Mine.

there.

A few days later, the tooth is gone. David chewing on a bloody handkerchief. "See?" he says. "Fuck Dad. I can take care of myself."

here.

The only thing that can take away this pain is a different kind of pain.

you.

Your face when you were sleeping. The only time I trusted you not to go away.

here.

No love, no pain.

there.

David's death, permanent on my skin. He joins the other scars. So he'll be with me always. So he can never leave.

here.

Again. A razor blade between my fingers. This old bully, resurrected. A promise to myself, broken.

Each cut, a good-bye. Each cut, the only truth I can speak.

The pressure, the break through skin, then the sting. The moment of fear mixed with anticipation, the moment before the blood blooms.

Each scar on my arm is a memory.

Then the relief. The sigh. The letting go. My pounding heart, the blood going whoosh inside my head.

Gone, gone. Everyone gone.

The moment of calm when I cross through the space in between pains.

Each scar is a point in time when everything else disappeared.

Now. Old scars reopened.

Whatever problem I had bleeds away.

I hide behind the blood.

I fall asleep before the shame sets in.

here.

NEON LIGHTS REFLECT OFF SCUFFED LINOLEUM FLOORS. Metal wheels squeak. Carts clatter. Phil Collins's eighties heartbreak song "Against All Odds" crackles over the loudspeaker. Dad hums along cheerfully, as if he's completely unaware that this is one of the saddest breakup songs ever written. I'm embarrassed that I even know this song. Dad's bad taste in music must have seeped into my subconscious over the course of my childhood.

"How can you just walk away from me?" Phil Collins sings.

How could you, Evie?

I'm leaning against the back of the shopping cart, following Dad through the aisles of the grocery store. Since my run-in with the cops, he's been overdoing it in the parenting department, as if making a sudden heroic effort to pay attention to me will make me behave the way he wants, as if watching TV next to each other on the couch will get me closer to becoming a miniature version of him. There's no use grounding me since I don't have a life, so he has made my punishment more "family time," but I cringe every time he says it. I don't know how he can justify calling the two of us a family.

The fresh cuts on my shoulder throb beneath their bandage, and my dad has no idea. Even after a couple of days, the wounds are still raw, still seeping. I woke up this morning and the old familiar shame was right there waiting for me, pounding in my head with every heartbeat. I had to throw away my favorite T-shirt, had to hide it in the bottom of my trash can so no one would see it. Nothing can get that much blood out.

I promised myself a year ago I wouldn't do this anymore. No one is worth this blood. No one is worth hurting myself over. But I still did it. I still thought it would fix something. But Evie is still gone and I am still empty.

"Marcus, where do you think we'd find marinated artichoke hearts?" Dad's looking at a list Monica gave him for dinner tonight, but neither of us know how to find anything outside the frozen food aisle.

"How would I know?" I say. I grab a jar of spaghetti sauce and a pack of noodles and throw them in the cart. That's all the cooking I know how to do.

"Eggplant?" he says. "Radicchio? Is this a joke?"

"Why don't we just order a pizza?"

"Monica is an amazing cook. It'll be worth it, I promise." He picks up a jar of capers and inspects it. "Damn, this is a good song."

"Phil Collins? Dad, you are so white."

"This was a big hit my senior year of high school."

"Did you slow dance to it at prom?"

He smiles and puts the jar of capers back on the shelf. "As a matter of fact, I did." He gets a faraway look on his face. He sways his hips to the music. "Ah, Gina Edwards. She was so fine."

"Gross," I say, but for a second, I imagine my dad, thirty years younger, with a sculpted Afro, big ears, an eighties-style tux and tacky boutonniere, an awkward teenager under a disco ball during the ugliest style period in history. That cheers me up a little.

It's Friday night, and I'm hanging out with my dad at the grocery store, but I am beyond caring about cool. At least I'm somewhere besides my room with the walls crushing in on me. At least there are things to look at and smell and hear, to distract my senses. I'll take anything to get out of my own head. Anything to drown out the spiraling thoughts in my mind, the scene on repeat, over and over, of Evie standing there and saying nothing.

The truth is, spending time with my dad the last few days hasn't been all that bad. I must really be losing my mind.

"You're the only one who really knew me at all."

Fuck you, Phil Collins. You are so not helping.

Dad's mouth is moving, but I can't hear what he's saying. My mind cannot comprehend his voice, does not recognize it without its usual tinge of anger and exasperation. Something is wrong with his face. It is too soft, too kind. His lips curl up at the edges.

Monica leans over and kisses him on the cheek. "Marcus, your dad is so funny," she says.

"Huh?" I say, poking at a purple vegetable I do not recognize.

"He was just telling me a story from when you were a kid."

"Remember that time we went camping?" Dad says, laughing. I shudder at the memory.

"We went camping one time," he says. "And that was enough to convince us to never do it again."

"What happened?" Monica asks.

"First of all, it rained. It started as soon as we pulled into the camping spot. I had never set up a tent before, but I was determined to do it. Renae suggested going home, but of course I would not admit defeat."

"Of course not," Monica says with a playful roll of her eyes. I study her face for a moment and see the glimmer of something real, even likable.

"I was going to succeed no matter who I took down with me," he says, and something warm and unexpected spreads in my chest. What is this new self-effacing humor? He meets my eyes for a moment, and I'm the one who looks away first.

Dad chuckles. "I tried to build a fire with wet wood for about two hours while everyone else hid in the tent."

"We had an okay time," I say. "Mom brought lots of books and games."

"Yeah," he says with a sudden sadness. "I remember hearing you all laughing. I could have joined you, but somehow I thought it was more important to build a stupid fire in the pouring rain."

Monica reaches over and puts her hand over his and they share a look between them that I never saw between him and my mother. Monica *gets* him. He's letting her get him.

I take a small bite of my dinner. It's good, like restaurant good. Way better than the frozen crap we usually stock.

"What do you think, William?" Monica says with a smile in her eyes. "Is now a good time?"

Dad takes a deep breath. "It's as good a time as any." He wipes his mouth with the cloth napkin from his lap. "Marcus," he begins. "Monica and I have something we want to tell you."

And just like that, I am numb. I have no feelings. Doors shut. I am closed for business.

"We're getting married!" Monica says, bursting with happiness.

What am I supposed to say? I want to warn her. She has no idea what she's getting herself into.

"Marcus," Dad says, "I would be honored if you'd be my best man."

"Okay," I say blankly, in shock. I don't know what I think. I don't know what I feel.

"I know this must be a huge surprise for you," Monica says. "And you probably have a lot of different feelings coming up."

Nope. No feelings. None at all.

"We love each other very much," Dad says, and even if it's true, it sounds like bullshit.

My phone rings. Perfect timing. I pull it out of my pocket and see a number I don't recognize.

"I have to get this," I say, standing up. Dad's dopey in-love face shows a glimmer of the more familiar angry-dad face.

"Hello?" I say as I walk out of the kitchen and into the living room.

"Marcus?" says a girl's voice.

"Yeah. Who's this?"

"My name's Kasey," she says. "I'm a friend of Evie's."

My heart stops. All the feelings I wasn't feeling a moment ago come rushing into my body at once like some kind of toxic storm. I feel everything there is to feel. I am light-headed. I need to sit down.

"How is she?" I ask, leaning against the wall. "Is she okay?"

"She's fine. She's great, actually."

Something releases inside my chest. I exhale and close my eyes. When I open them, tears cut a river down my cheeks.

"She wants to see you."

"Why didn't she call me herself?"

"She wants to talk to you, but she didn't want to do it over the phone." The voice named Kasey sighs. "Do you want to talk to her or not?"

"Yes," I say. "Yes." A million times, yes.

A tiny glimmer of hope. The world stops ending.

you.

SO MUCH SPOKEN IN WHISPERS. A SECRET LANGUAGE between us.

You said, "You see me." And in those moments, I believed you. When your shoulders would fall away from your ears. When you would close your eyes and breathe into my neck, and we'd curve around each other like swans, and I would find the places made for my lips.

Supposedly, swans mate for life. When they kiss, their necks form the shape of a heart.

But a swan song is not a love song. It is good-bye. It is a last act, a final performance.

Does a swan really sing when it dies? Is its pain really that beautiful?

here.

I'M WALKING TOWARD A COFFEE SHOP IN DOWNTOWN Berkeley, the kind of chain Evie and I would never have gone to.

I feel her before I see her. The back of my neck tingles. My eyes find her at a table in the corner, staring at me. My feet don't feel the ground as I walk the miles it takes to get to her. Her smile is nervous. She seems to be shaking as she stands up to hug me. The hug ends before I even have a chance to feel her in my arms, before I have a chance to smell her. My body stings with her absence.

She sits down and so do I. "Do you want to get something?" she says.

"No, I'm fine," I say. "What are you having?"

"Green tea."

"That's new."

"Yeah, I'm trying not to do coffee anymore."

"Why?"

She shrugs. "Trying to be healthy, I guess."

"Me, too," I say.

"Yeah?"

"Yeah."

Evie's toned down her look in the few weeks since her coma. She's in a simple T-shirt and jeans, her face is bare of makeup, and her short blond hair is swept casually to the side. The hardness she had cultivated before is nowhere to be found. She's more beautiful than ever.

"You look good," I say. "Healthy."

"I've been swimming a lot," she says. "You cut your hair."

"I needed a change."

She takes a sip of her tea in the silence that follows. I wish I had bought a drink so I'd have something to do with my hands.

"This small talk feels weird," Evie finally says. "We never had to do small talk."

"So let's stop talking small."

She holds her breath for a moment before speaking. "I'm sorry it's taken me so long to contact you. I know you must have been worried. It was cruel of me to disappear like that without an explanation."

I say nothing. I wait for more.

"Even now, I can't really explain it." She's looking at her hands. "When I woke up from the coma, the first thought on my mind was that I needed space. Not just from you, from everything that reminded me of cancer, of my life after cancer, everything that reminded me of getting high."

"You needed to run away," I say.

"No, Marcus," she says firmly, looking up from her hands. Her pale blue eyes burn into mine. "I needed to stop running."

"You could have told me," I say. "I would have understood. You could have trusted me."

She shakes her head.

"You didn't trust me?"

"No. It's not that." She suddenly looks so innocent, so lost. "I didn't trust myself. I knew if I saw you, I'd fall back into my old ways."

"But I wouldn't let you. If I knew that's what you wanted. I'd help you, Evie."

"That's not something you can control. It's not up to you."

I shake my head. "I don't understand."

"I don't have everything figured out yet. But I think you inspire something in me." She looks down. She cannot meet my eyes. "Something reckless."

"You're blaming this on me?"

"No. It's—" She searches for words. "It's how I react to you."

"That doesn't make any sense."

She stares at her tea, so rigid, so still, and I am a hurricane.

"You know my parents wanted to press charges against you?" she finally says. "They wanted to believe everything was your fault. I managed to convince them you didn't know anything about the pills."

"I didn't."

"Right. So you're off the hook. You avoided the wrath of the Whinsetts." She's trying to be funny, but I cannot think of a worse time for humor.

"What happened?" I say. "How could you let it get that far?"

She sighs. "My dad's father was a horrible alcoholic, and so was his grandfather. I never met either of them. They both died young. That's why my dad doesn't drink, why there's never been any booze in our house. Dad vowed never to drink because of them. The disease is in my blood," she says, "before drugs or alcohol even entered my body. I can't ever get away from it. It's like I was programmed to get addicted as soon as I tried something."

We're both quiet for a minute. Even though I know addiction can be hereditary, it seems like such a convenient excuse. If it has everything to do with your family, why did Evie catch it and I didn't?

Evie laughs a tired, ironic laugh. "What is it with me and diseases?"

I shake my head slowly. I cannot stop shaking my head. It is the only movement that feels right. "How could I not have known you were high all those times? How could I be so stupid?"

"There's no way you could have known. I did everything I could to hide it from you. From everyone."

"I should have noticed the signs. I know what they look like. There were so many."

"Marcus, don't."

"The flu? Who gets the fucking flu in June?"

"That's over now."

"I could have helped you. I wanted to help you."

"I know."

"I can help you now."

That's when I notice the tears in her eyes, her bottom lip trembling.

"I'm changing, too," I say. "I quit smoking pot. I have a really great internship this summer."

"I'm happy for you," she says sadly.

"We can help each other."

"You can't save me, Marcus."

"We can save each other."

"No," she says. "We can't."

"Why not?"

"That's just not how it works."

Silence. A silence so loud it kills me.

Evie sits up straight and I can tell it's taking all her strength to look at me. "My one priority right now is to stay sober," she says with a rehearsed strength in her voice. "I have to let go of everything that might get in the way of my doing that."

"So you're letting go of me?"

"I have to take care of myself now," she says without feeling, as if it's a line, pumped into her by some ventriloquist. "I can't see you anymore."

"Do you still love me?" I demand.

"Marcus, don't."

"I have a right to ask that. I have a right to know."

"And I have a right to not answer."

My shoulders tense, the muscles in my arms go rigid. Somewhere deep down, I know I still love the girl in front of me. But all I can feel right now is disgust, fury. "I used to think you were the bravest person I ever met."

She looks away.

"But maybe I was wrong." I want to hurt her. I want to tear her apart. "Maybe you're a coward like everyone else."

"Stop it."

"Only a coward could throw someone away like this."

"Marcus, stop."

"If you love someone, you stick around. No matter what." I know I'm raising my voice, I know people are looking, but I don't care.

"Please go," she whispers.

"No." I pound my fist on the table. Her cup of tea spills and drenches my lap, not hers.

"Just go!" Evie yells. "Leave me alone!" Everyone in the café looks in our direction. A few bodies lean toward us, ready to protect the sweet-looking girl from the thug across from her. Of course everyone would assume it's me who hurt her.

"Fine," I say. "I'm going." I stand up. "You're really good at this, aren't you?"

"Good at what?" she mutters, unable to meet my eye.

"Breaking people's hearts."

Then I walk out the door.

I need to rage. I need to slam into people. I need to go someplace so loud it will drown everything else out.

So I drive to the one place I know I can count on for this kind of diversion: 924 Gilman, the all-ages punk club in Berkeley where bands like Green Day and AFI got their start, before they sold out and made millions.

The handwritten sign in front of the club says tonight is a metal-core showcase, featuring bands I've never heard of. The people milling around outside are the usual mix ranging from Urban Outfitters pseudohipsters to Dumpster-diving gutter punks who look halfway to homeless. As usual, I am the only nonwhite person here, as I am at most shows I go to. By now, I am used to being the token black guy, despite living in an area full of black people. But the scenes don't mix much, and I'm even more of an outsider with the black kids than I am here.

I walk through a cloud of cigarette smoke to buy my ticket and notice a girl with long bright-green hair and a lip ring checking me out. An old spark ignites and the warmth feels better than anything I've felt in a long time.

"Hey," I say. "Do you have an extra smoke?" Her eyes are lined with dark purple. The rings in her ears are thick plugs of wood. She's cute, but I can't help but compare her to Evie, how Evie's beauty was so natural, how she didn't have to try so hard to be cool.

"For you, my dear," the girl says. "Anything." She puts a new cigarette in her mouth along with the one she's already smoking, lights it, and places it between my lips.

"Got anything stronger?" I say, and she grins. She takes my hand and I follow her.

We smoke a bowl behind a boarded-up warehouse a couple blocks away from the club. Gilman has a strict no drugs and alcohol policy, but they must know at least half of the people at the shows are wasted. The girl's name is Amber and she's from San Leandro. I lie and tell her I just graduated from Oakland Tech.

We don't talk much as we pass the pipe back and forth. The more I look at her, the more I can tell this isn't really her style. Her large-gauge earrings are fakes—I can see the part going through her ear is actually a normal-sized piercing. Her shirt is newly ripped. Her scalp is still green from the recent dye job.

A wave of sadness hits me so hard it makes me sick to my stomach. I don't want to do this. Not this bullshit. Not here. Not with her, not with anyone who's not Evie. But then she reaches over and pulls me close, puts her mouth close to my ear, says, "Want to go see the show?" and I can't think of how to tell her no.

The club is dark and the music is loud and pounding. The vocalist screams into the mic and he could be talking gibberish for all I know. It doesn't matter what he's saying, just how it sounds, how it feels, how the rage and anger pulses through the crowd and catches like wildfire. People are pushing and thrashing in front of the stage, running into each other, knocking each other over, taking out their aggression on strangers and friends. Are they really that angry, all these stomping white kids with tattoos and bulging neck veins? What are they so angry about? Does it even matter?

I want to run into the middle of it. I want to get bruised and beaten by these people I don't know. Amber hangs back while I throw myself into the pit. I close my eyes and join the jabbing elbows and shoulders, the hands pushing, the bodies slamming. But none of it hurts, not really, not in the way that counts.

The pit is a frenzy of men, half of them shirtless, running around in circles until they crash into another's orbit, hot skin on skin, sweat mixing. We touch but never make eye contact. It looks like rage. It looks like anger. But maybe that's not all it is. Maybe it's the only way some people can figure out how to touch, how to throw themselves into another person without really getting hurt.

After a few songs, I am panting and drenched with sweat, not all of it mine. All the songs sound the same—same beat, same three chords, same unintelligible screaming—but I don't care. I stand on the edge to catch my breath. Blood races through me like electricity. I need to do something with this adrenaline. I'm not done, not spent.

A hand grabs mine and pulls me into the shadows against the wall. Lips and a tongue that taste like smoke and cinnamon.

Amber pulls me to her, presses her body against mine. "Do you have a car?" she says.

I nod.

"Take me there," she says, even more breathless than me.

We are silent as we fumble around in the car to put our clothes back on. I kept my shirt on so she wouldn't see the fresh cuts on my shoulder, and I can feel the sting of wounds reopened. The stain of blood on my shirt shimmers in the darkness, evidence of my cracking open. I am so tired—posthigh, postmosh, postsex—and all I want to do is curl into my bed and sleep. But there's a girl next to me pulling a shirt over her head. There's a sick, empty feeling in my stomach telling me I made a huge mistake. We just did one of the most intimate things two people can do, but I don't think I've ever felt so lonely.

Amber puts on a fresh coat of bright red lipstick, then pulls out her phone and starts texting. We are inches apart, but it's like I'm not even there.

"So," I say.

"Hold on," she says, holding up a finger to silence me. Her phone buzzes with a new text, she types something back, then puts the phone in her purse. She looks at me and smiles the kind of smile you'd give someone ringing up your groceries.

"That was fun," she says.

"Can I call you some time?" I think that's what I'm supposed to say.

She laughs. "You're really cute, Marcus. But I don't want a boyfriend or anything. I'm leaving for Vassar in like two months and I'm traveling most of the summer."

"Oh."

"I'm gonna go now, okay?" she says, opening the door. She leans over and gives me a peck on the cheek. "So cute." She climbs out of the car and closes the door, leaving me in the backseat, sticky with the sweat of so many strangers.

When I get home, I take a shower and wash the memory of this night off me. But I also have the munchies, so I stop in the kitchen to grab some food before I head upstairs. I hear footsteps on the stairs, and I throw my sweatshirt over my head just in time so Dad won't see the bloodstains on my shirt.

He's humming as he enters the kitchen, in pajama pants with no shirt on. The tuft of tight curls on his chest has started to gray, and his belly is rounder than I remember it.

He startles when he sees me. "Oh, Marcus," he says, and I can tell he's embarrassed. "Hi."

"Hey, Dad."

"I'm getting a snack," he says.

"Okay."

"I guess I should tell you that Monica is sleeping over."

Gross. My dad just got laid.

"You don't have to tell me that. Seriously."

"No, I do. This is your home, too. I want to be open and honest with you."

"There's such a thing as being too open and honest."

He chuckles as he grabs a bottle of water and some food out of the fridge. I pretend not to watch him as he sets it out nicely on a tray, fussing over the placement of each thing. He seems more human in this moment than I remember him being in a long time, so not like my father.

"All you need is a little vase and a flower," I say. "Then you could get a job delivering room service."

"I'll keep that in mind if this whole judge thing doesn't work out."

"It's important to have something to fall back on."

"Ha."

I wonder what my dad would think about my one-night stand. I wonder how he feels about the ones he used to have before he got serious with Monica. I wonder how he feels now that they're supposedly going to be over.

No, not going to go there.

"Well, good night," Dad says, taking his tray of water and snacks.

He takes a few steps toward the door, then I surprise myself by saying, "Dad, wait." He turns around. "Can I ask you something?"

"Sure." He sets the tray down on the counter.

"What's it like having Mom back here? What's it like for you?"

He's as surprised as I am by the question, and it takes him a few seconds to answer. "Well, I'm glad you two are starting to talk again."

"But what's it like for *you*? Aren't you pissed?"

"To be honest, we get along a lot better now than we ever did married."

"But aren't you mad at her? I mean, she took all that money, for one thing."

He sighs. "She was going to get half of it in the divorce anyway."

"How can you forgive her so easy? Don't you hate her?"

He thinks for a moment, like he's seriously considering the question. "I hate what she did," he finally says. "I hate that she left you. But she did what she thought she had to do. She didn't think she had any other choice."

"People always have a choice," I say.

"Maybe. But a lot of times, they don't know it."

"That's their fault."

"It's more complicated than that, Marcus. People are complicated. Your mom was miserable, and I know I had a lot to do with that." He looks me in the eyes, searching for understanding.

"When you love someone," he continues, "you're supposed to bring out the best in each other. I brought out the worst in your mom."

"Did she bring out the worst in you?"

He thinks for a moment. "To be honest, I don't think I really gave her a chance to bring out much of anything in me. You may not have noticed, but I haven't been the most emotionally available man in the world." If I respond, if I nod, that means I accept this veiled attempt at an apology. But I'm not ready for this to be how we talk to each other. I'm not ready to accept this version of my dad who says things the way they are instead of ignoring them.

"Your mom and I weren't right for each other," he says. "We both know that, and we've made peace with it. She's doing really well now, Marcus. And she really loves you."

I shrug.

"Sometimes people's actions don't always match their intentions," he says. "Sometimes people do things backward, and it takes doing the wrong thing to bring them to a place where they can do the right thing. She's trying to do the right thing. I really hope you decide to give her another chance."

I can't help but laugh at how ridiculous this night has turned out. "Do you have a fever?" I say. "You're not yourself. Do you think Monica maybe slipped something in your drink?"

"Maybe." Dad smiles. "I hope it doesn't wear off anytime soon."

"Yeah, me too," I say, then immediately regret it. This is what hurts—this softness, this exposure—not the bruises from slamming into people in the pit.

Or is it this I want more of? Is this the kind of real connection I've been craving? If it is, then why is it so painful?

We stand in awkward silence, neither of us knowing how to acknowledge the excruciatingly tender moment.

"Well, good night," Dad says, picking up the tray, and I breathe a sigh of relief.

"Yeah," I say. "Good night." And a part of me stretches thin as he walks away. A part of me wants him to turn around and come back.

you.

I'M TRYING TO GET OVER YOU, BUT IT'S NOT WORKING. Everywhere I turn, I see you. My breath catches in my throat and I almost say your name, but then the figure turns around and it's a stranger.

But how different are they, really? How well did I know you compared to these random women on the street? I have no clue how to decipher the truth from your fictions. Is something less true when spoken between lies? Do words lose their meaning when doused in alcohol or tangled in some other drug?

Your eyes, those were not lies. Your skin. Your touch. They way your fingertips whispered on the back of my neck. The way you fell into me and let me carry you. Those rare moments when your body softened and you released your burdens.

But maybe it had nothing to do with me. How often were we actually sober together? Does our love even count? Maybe your feelings were only chemical concoctions. Maybe you never loved me at all; maybe you fell in love with your own chemistry.

Who did I fall in love with? A ghost? My own projections onto the shell of you? Who was I talking to all those times I thought I was pouring into you, when I told you secrets I never told anyone? What does it mean that I finally felt safe? What does it mean that you said you did, too?

Evie, I don't know if I miss you or my fantasy of you. I remember what you look like, how you felt in my arms; I remember the physical weight of you, the tangible things, the things that could not be faked. But there is something else, a kind of smoke, the weightless stuff that fills you up—that is what I'm not sure about. There's a taste of it on my tongue, a residue of memory, but I don't know if it's you or myself I am tasting.

It's not even a question of whether or not we were good for each other. It's a question of whether we existed at all.

here.

I'M WALKING IN FRONT, TAKING LONG STEPS UP THE STEEP trail. I can tell I'm going a little too fast, that Mom is struggling to keep up, but I don't care. I'm still not ready to admit to myself that I agreed to go hiking with the woman I vowed to never forgive or let back into my life.

But loneliness does weird things to people. She called at exactly the right time. My guard was down. I wanted to say yes to something. Anything.

The trail cuts through the yellow-brown grass of the scorched East Bay hills under a periodic canopy of oak, madrona, and eucalyptus, carved into the side of the hill by a deep ravine. It is so silent out here, so still. A light breeze rustles the leaves, but it is not so much movement as it is a variation of stillness.

"So what are we supposed to talk about?" I say to break the silence.

"I don't know," Mom says from behind me, a little out of breath. "What do you want to talk about?"

I walk even faster. I am taking more than a slight pleasure in her struggle to keep up with me. "Am I supposed to fill you in on every little thing that's happened since you left? Because I'm not going to do that."

"Okay."

"I don't want to talk about the past."

"So don't."

"Fine."

We make it to the top of an overlook, and I stop for a moment to take in the view of rolling hills that opens up to the east, grazing cows dotting the landscape. "Isn't this beautiful?" Mom says, panting slightly, but I walk again before she has a chance to catch her breath.

"Marcus," she says. I keep walking. "Marcus, wait."

I stop because I'm tired, too. We're in a patch of shade. There's a perfect bench on the side of the trail, but I won't sit down and admit defeat.

"This isn't a race, you know," Mom says.

"I'm not racing," I say. "I'm trying to get some exercise."

She sits down on the bench and I fight the urge to join her. "You think if you walk fast enough, you won't have to talk to me?" she says.

I say nothing. I wipe the sweat off my brow, but some drips into my eyes. It stings, blinding me for a moment.

"What are you afraid of?"

"I'm not afraid."

She pats the space next to her on the bench. "Have a seat. Rest awhile."

"I'm fine standing."

"Tell me something, Marcus."

"Like what?"

"Like anything. What are you obsessed with these days?"

What a strange choice of words.

"Name the first thing that comes to you," she says.

"Evie." The forbidden word comes out of my mouth before I have a chance to stop it, as if it has a mind of its own, as if it wanted to be said.

"Tell me about this Evie."

If I speak out here, without the walls and streets to hear me, maybe it won't count. Maybe these hills are a place we can throw our words to the wind and they'll blow away without a trace.

"She was my girlfriend," I say, sitting on the bench next to my mother. I feel an immediate relief, a weight being lifted, and I don't know if it's from the sitting or the speaking. Mom's eyes are on me, but I look down at the ground, kicking a stick with my boot. "We were in love. She was everything."

"And now?"

I look at her, and the warmth and tenderness in her eyes melts me, turns me into the child who still trusted her. I feel the heat of tears in my eyes.

"And now she's gone," I say, choking a little on my words. "She got hooked on pills and wouldn't let me help her. She almost died." And now I'm crying, really crying, as if I've saved up my tears from all the years I never did this, never talked to my mom about what's going on, never gave her my pain because she was so busy carrying David's, so busy carrying her own. Her arm is around me and I let her pull me against her. "But she's alive," I say. I wipe my nose and sit up. "She's alive and sober and refuses to see me. Like I'm some kind of poison. Like she thinks I'm going to hurt her. I would never hurt her. All I ever wanted was for her to be happy."

"Maybe this has nothing to do with you, Marcus," Mom says gently. "Maybe there are things she needs to do on her own."

"But she still loves me. I know she does. If she didn't, I think I could accept it. I could let her go. But I can't."

"Maybe," Mom says, and a small part of me thinks I should be angry at her calmness, at her defending Evie without even knowing her or our situation. But a greater part of me is so grateful to be speaking. "She needs to go through what she needs to go through," Mom says. "She needs to figure out her own way to heal."

"I know," I whimper, sniffling on my tears. I feel like a child, but it's not an entirely bad feeling.

"I think if you really love her, you need to let her do that, even if it means being away from you. She needs to do it on her own terms."

"Fuck her own terms," I say pathetically.

"I know," she says. "Fuck people whose needs don't match ours. Fuck people who need space."

"Like you did."

"Like I did," she says. After a moment, she adds, "But I did it all wrong, Marcus. I fucked up. You have every right to be mad at me."

"Fuck you, Mom," I say, but I'm almost smiling.

"Fuck everybody," she says.

"God, what's wrong with me?" I say as I stand up. I offer my hand and she takes it. "Why do I keep getting mixed up with women like you two?"

"Maybe we have something to teach you."

We start walking, out of the shade and back into the sunlight. "Like what?" I say. "Stay away from crazy blond chicks?"

"Yeah," Mom says, and I can hear the smile in her voice. "That's probably it."

We start walking, this time side by side, at the same pace.

After a few minutes, Mom speaks: "How are you, Marcus? How are you *really*?"

"Fine," I say, but I already know she's not going to accept that answer.

"Come on. Talk to me. What's the worst thing that could happen?"

You could leave. You could stay.

"What are you doing these days?" she says. "School's over, you don't have a job. What do you do with your time?"

"I'm going to do that internship with Dad."

"You know what I mean."

I try to think of something to say that will satisfy her, but I can think of nothing.

Nothing. That's what I'm doing. That's what my life is made out of.

"I don't know," I say. "Not much."

"Is she really worth it?"

I say nothing. She doesn't even know Evie. She barely knows me. What makes her think she's figured me out?

"Is this girl worth throwing your whole summer away? Is she worth torturing yourself and putting your life on hold while you wait for her to come back?"

I shrug. I feel like I should be angry, but I'm not. I'm strangely calm. I'm interested in what Mom has to say.

"It's like you're making yourself miserable to get back at her," she says. "But who exactly are you punishing? Certainly not her."

"Are you, like, practicing to become a motivational speaker or something?" I say.

"I just don't like seeing you give up on life because of some girl."

"She's not just some girl."

"Does that really change anything?"

I shrug because I don't want to admit out loud that she's right. My mother—this woman who left her husband and two sons when things got too hard—is giving me advice. But I guess she does know something about putting life on hold for other people. She knows about losing herself. She knows about loneliness.

"Your dad's new girlfriend seems nice," she says.

"Can we just not talk for a while? Please?"

"Sure, honey. Of course."

I listen to the pebbles crunch beneath our feet. This is how sand is made—hundreds and thousands and millions of footsteps, years and decades and centuries of wind and rain and ice and earthquakes. Life rubbing up against something hard, wearing it down, turning it into tiny versions of itself.

In a couple of hours, I will be back down at sea level, back in my house, surrounded by the same things, with the same empty summer spread out before me.

I can't go back to that. I can't.

here.

THE FIRST DAY OF MY INTERNSHIP AT DAD'S OFFICE WENT as good as it could have, I guess. I blended in with the other glassy-eyed morning commuters in button-up shirts and slacks, swaying with the motion of the BART train to San Francisco. At eight thirty a.m., it was already in the upper eighties as I filed out of the Civic Center station, walked through the gauntlet of panhandlers and hustlers without making eye contact with anyone, passed through the metal detectors to get into the courthouse, and listened to the echo of my footsteps join others as I found my way to Dad's office through the marble halls. His assistant, Fletcher, showed me around and then parked me in front of a computer with a pile of files to scan and upload. Dad made a three-minute appearance between meetings, time enough to say hi and pat me on the back.

Now, nine hours later, I am on the BART train again, my eyes aching from looking at the computer screen, my hands dry from handling so much paper, my white shirt stained with sweat. This is my first taste of a respectable adult life: a commute, a desk, a few hours of mostly mind-numbing tasks, small talk by the coffee-maker. The most exciting thing that happens all day is walking through a cloud of crack smoke and barely avoiding stepping in a pile of human shit on the sidewalk. I'm on the train with a bunch of grumpy, overheated strangers forced to stand after a long day of work. We crush each other, slam wet armpits into faces. The men sitting in the seats by the door pretend not to see either the pregnant woman standing right in front of them or the sign that tells them to give up their seat to her.

I thought I saw Evie on the street, but it was one of the half-clothed and zombie-eyed prostitutes wandering down the hill from the Tenderloin district. I thought I saw her in the courthouse, a beautiful attorney in a pencil skirt and high heels. I thought I saw her on the train, a young summer intern like me, trying to start a life, trying to become someone who matters. No matter what I do or where I go, she follows me.

So now what? How do I outrun the ghost of someone who's still living?

I decide to get off at the MacArthur station and walk the three miles home because I have nothing else I want to do. My job covered the day, but there is still the night to fill.

The area outside the station has a familiar smell of cheap incense. That guy with the haggard dreads and Rasta shirt has been sitting in that same spot for as long as I can remember. I bet it's a front for drugs. The old me might ask him what he's holding.

The old me might see a solution in getting high, in running away. It is tempting. But after all this time trying, I know it accomplishes nothing. It certainly won't bring Evie back.

It is too hot for incense. The air is already stifling. I overheard someone on the train saying Oakland was supposed to get up to ninety-five today. The news says to stay indoors because of the dangerously bad air quality. The sky is hazy and stings the eyes because of forest fires burning up north. There's a water shortage. Alameda and surrounding counties have forbidden the watering of lawns. Even rich Piedmont grass is turning yellow. Down here, everyone is sweating, miserable, and cranky. Young black men, shirtless, ride bikes around in lazy circles, trying to create their own wind.

This is the kind of heat that kills people. This is the kind of weather that can make people crazy.

Crazy.

I must be going crazy.

Because standing on the sidewalk across the street, surrounded by a cloud of smoke, is Evie. In broad daylight during rush hour, on a hot day of car exhaust and baking concrete. On a day of sweating into long-sleeved shirts with tight-buttoned cuffs. On a day of filing papers and pressing buttons, marble hallways, mahogany furniture.

What a strange place for a ghost to appear, in a crowd of mismatched people outside a church, smoking cigarettes and holding Styrofoam cups. An old biker in a frayed leather vest looks at his watch and speaks words I cannot hear. People throw their cigarettes into the street and file down a set of stairs into a base-ment. Evie says something to a blue-haired woman old enough to be her grandmother.

"Evie!" I yell across the street. "Wait!" But the speeding cars steal my words.

Cars honk and tires screech as I run across the street. I don't check to see if anyone's coming. There is only my destination. There is only the line of my path there. Two dimensions. The cars can wait.

I run down the stairs and find myself in an empty, half-lit hallway, at least twenty degrees cooler than the air outside. A fluo-rescent light flickers on stained gray walls. I'm underground. This could be a tunnel, a cave, a catacomb. But it is only a church base-ment. It smells like linoleum, bleach, and burned coffee. There were so many people on the street, but now they're gone, just like that, disappeared into thin air. Ghosts, all of them.

I open the door in front of me, but it is just a dusty supply closet. The next door is an empty bathroom. The next door is locked. I turn the corner and there are two staircases, more doors, more corners. A big kitchen, a huge dining room, the smell of old gravy. Empty, all of it. So much space for nothing. The people from the sidewalk, gone. Lost. Evie, swept away with them.

Or maybe they were never there at all. Maybe the sun is get-ting to me. Maybe this is what heatstroke feels like, hallucinations and a heart thumping out of my chest. I walk up a set of stairs to the back of a dark and empty chapel, the pews lined up straight and perfect, the creepy stained glass of a bloody, heartbroken Jesus on the cross glaring down at me, the glass illuminated Technicolor by the hot Oakland sun. Everything else is dark and shadowed except him up there, tortured and untouchable, reminding everyone who sees him how much they break his heart.

I haven't been in a church since David's funeral.

So many ghosts. So many fucking ghosts.

I turn around and stumble down the stairs, dizzy. There are too many doors, too many twists and turns. This door is locked. That room is empty. Where do people go when they disappear?

Something in the corner of my eye. Movement in the hall. Someone walking by, in a direction I haven't been yet. Something human shaped. I go. I run.

The back of someone slipping through a door. Muted voices escape before the door closes, a group recitation, a monotone chant. Some sort of ritual. Ghosts rising from the dead.

I open the door and look inside. Folding chairs in rows, people facing a podium, someone reading from a battered old blue book. Big posters with lists on the walls. A framed picture of an old white guy with a long face. I scan the crowd for Evie. Old people, young people, white and black and brown, upscale and haggard and everything in between. But no Evie. These are the people she was with on the sidewalk, I'm sure of it.

An old hippie-looking guy sitting by the door sees me and smiles a creepy cult smile. "Welcome," he whispers. "Glad you're here." Then he motions for me to sit in the empty seat next to him. I turn around and run. Through the labyrinth of cool, empty halls. Up the stairs and back into the heat.

I'm going crazy. This isn't about love anymore. This is obsession. This is nuts. Sane people don't run across traffic to follow groups of weird strangers. They don't go chasing hallucinations around church basements or go bursting into cult meetings.

Do normal people know when they're going crazy? Is this what the beginning of madness feels like?

My room is dark. I have one candle burning. I lie on my couch watching the flame. My shirt is off and the light of the candle flickers on my rib cage. I can almost feel Evie's soft lips brushing my skin.

My phone buzzes with a new text, but I don't bother to look at it. I know it's Mom. She's the only one who ever texts me anymore. I don't know what happened to me on our hike the other day, but I was weak; I let down my guard. Maybe it was the sun and fresh air and being away from the city, maybe the trees did something to me. Maybe I was desperate.

All I can motivate myself to do is water David's plants. I trim the dead leaves. There seem to be more than usual, shriveled and yellow. A few pots have developed a white mold in the soil. No matter what I do, the plants keep dying.

I'm well acquainted with sadness. I know it's what I've been trying to fight all this time with cutting, with drugs. But now my drugs are gone and the fresh cuts on my shoulder have scabbed over. I'm growing new skin. I've thrown my pipes and rolling papers and lighters away; I've thrown away my razor blades. And now there's a new feeling surfacing, something sharper breaking through, not the sadness I'm used to.

Depression is like fog, like a heavy smoke that permeates everything, that sneaks into all the cracks of me and weighs me down. Everything pales and darkens. Everything moves slower. But this other feeling is like something cutting through all that. Like lightning. Like fire. Like claws scraping. Fangs biting. Sharp and hot and fast. It comes from the same place, but it takes a detour.

I am angry. I am furious. And even though the feeling is new, it seems to already know me, like I have been carrying it for years, like it has been watching me all this time, planning its attack, gaining strength, curating its collection of resentments until the point of saturation, until there's no room for any more deception and desertion and disappointment, until I'm full, until I am holding all the pain I can handle, until all the different pains fuse together and become one huge evil pulsing inside me.

I look at my left shoulder, at the old scars crisscrossed with new ones, and I am disgusted.

I don't know who I miss more, David or Evie. The loss of them mixes together and envelops me. I cannot tell the pains apart. They turn into concrete, and I am stuck inside it, immobile, my arms caught midstretch, my mouth wide, screaming. And then it all shatters, rock flying, and my heart breaks in a million different ways.

I am done. I am done being deceived. I am done believing in people. I am done with the foolishness of having hope. I look at my scars and renew my vow to never let anyone in again, like I promised a year ago when David died. But love made me weak. It made me break my promise. It let the pain back in.

I pick up my phone, send a text to my mom: *Stop texting. Stop calling. I don't want to see you again.* I throw my phone across the room.

I look back at the flame. I breathe. My world is only as big as this weak light.

there.

THE FIRST TEXT READS: *I DID IT AL WRONGH I LET HIM WNN*

Five minutes later: *yr good marcus dont frget yr good*

One minute later: *i wasnt good enohg*

Seven minutes later: *its goin to hurt im sory brothr*

I keep redialing David's number as I drive to his house, but he never answers. He has sent me plenty of weird texts before, probably written while he's out of his mind high, but this feels different.

His ex-girlfriend has been calling me for a week, leaving increasingly angry messages on my voice mail demanding I get David out of the apartment. The lease is in her name and she's finally moving out. She hasn't stayed there in more than two months. Her last message threatened to call the cops if he wasn't gone by that weekend.

It's the middle of the day, in the middle of summer. It's hot and windy, and I'm hungover. Even the wind is hot. I slept with a girl I met at a Templeton party whose name I don't remember. I had an empty, sour feeling in my stomach when I woke up that told me nothing good was going to come out of this day.

The hallway of the run-down apartment building smells like cooking grease and cigarette smoke. Half of the lights are out, and the dark-red carpet is stained in too many places to count. I walk slowly down the hall at first, then something tells me to start running.

I don't knock. Somehow I already knew there would be no answer. Somehow I knew the door would be unlocked.

But I didn't know what to expect when I opened the door. I didn't know I'd find the apartment completely empty of furniture, with several windows open, trash and papers piled into corners by the wind. A small whirlwind of dust bunnies dances in the center of the kitchen floor, and I stand there transfixed for nearly a minute, watching them move. But then the world shudders open, and I notice the smell of rotting food, the mold-covered dishes piled in the swampy sink, the empty food cans and other garbage piled on the counter. I flip a light switch, but nothing happens. I try another. Nothing.

"David," I say, because it is what you do when you're looking for someone, even though I already know he will not answer.

It is two days after I let David into the house to steal stuff, two days of trying to convince myself he was only looking for money and things to sell.

Everything is quiet when I open the bathroom door. It's an odd feeling to see the worst thing imaginable and not be surprised. Someone pressed the pause button on the world, and everything is strangely still and peaceful. The small bathroom window lets in a weak orange light. Everything is soft.

My brother is on the floor, lodged between the wall and the toilet. I wonder how he got there. I imagine him pushing himself into the tiny space, making himself as small as possible. He is so skinny, it would not have been difficult.

For a second, I think maybe it isn't him. This body isn't David. Someone else with his arms and legs could have snuck in and replaced him.

It is warm inside the apartment, at least eighty degrees. Warm blood has a unique smell. Like meat. Like metal.

The floor is a pool of red. There is no dry surface left, and it bothers me that I can't remember the original color of the tile. Was it white? Gray? Beige? It would have to be replaced now, for sure. No way can you get bloodstains out of grout.

He's in his boxer shorts. Maybe he had been hot. Maybe he didn't want to get his clothes dirty. His shorts are blue with white snowflakes on them. I have the same ones buried somewhere deep in my dresser. I do not wear them. I thought they were ridiculous when we got matching three-packs for Christmas three years ago, Mom's last Christmas with us. David and I had woken up late, hungover from a Christmas Eve party the night before. Mom was already drunk on Irish coffees. Dad grudgingly came downstairs. Mom turned on the Christmas music too loud as we opened the presents as quickly as possible. I don't remember what else we got. I remember the three of us going back upstairs when it was over, David and I to our beds to continue sleeping, Dad to his office to work, leaving Mom by the tree to deal with the mess of wrapping paper.

Who is going to deal with this mess? Whose job will it be to clean this up?

David's hand rests on his leg, Dad's gun still in its grip. He could have just OD'd. He could have let himself go to sleep—painlessly, clean.

David never did anything by accident. There was a reason he wanted to make such a mess. There was a reason he needed to use Dad's gun. There was a reason he went through the trouble of stealing it.

He needed Dad to be here. He needed Dad to know both of their fingers were on the trigger.

The gun is strangely clean, even though everything else in the room is splattered with blood.

Blood. It is my brother's blood. It is pieces of David's brilliant, useless brain all over the walls.

I scream into the silence until the police come.

you.

EVIE, I'M LOSING YOU. THE MEMORIES OF US ARE FADING. They're less crisp. Muted. Echoes, wave ripples, expanding orbits.

The place where I keep a home for you is still here, warm, waiting. But there are other places that need to be tended to, haunted rooms that need to be cleaned out. Ghosts that need to be dealt with.

Other memories are taking over. They're bullying their way in, pushing you out. I try to hold on, but your hands are so small. You are doing other things. I can't hold on if you keep letting go.

You are ahead, moving forward, at a steady pace. I am running after you, but we are on different paths. I will never reach you like this. We will never touch by my chasing you.

here.

MOM'S BEEN TEXTING AND LEAVING VOICE MAILS, EVEN after my text telling her to leave me alone. Dad's been trying to talk to me, too. He begged me to join him and Monica for lunch today, and I had to go to make him shut up.

"Isn't this nice?" he says as we walk down Market Street to the restaurant a few blocks away from Civic Center. "Look at us—two professional men going to lunch downtown." He is artificially jolly. He pretends not to see the guy passed out on the sidewalk in front of us.

Monica has turned out to be one of those people who makes too much eye contact. She hugs me when we arrive to the restaurant. The huge diamond on her engagement ring sparkles indecently. After a few valiant tries to get me to talk, she finally lets me eat my veggie burger in silence while I read the depressing current events on my phone's news app. She and Dad spend the meal deep in conversation, but I don't hear anything they say.

As we wait for the bill and my dad goes to the restroom, she tries one last time. "Marcus," she says, "your dad says you've been a little down lately. I know sometimes it's hard to talk to your parents about certain things, but maybe it could be easier with someone who isn't family. At least, not yet." She winks. "Is there anything you want to talk about? Maybe I can help?"

I don't speak for a full minute, I'm in so much shock. I'm not sure if I should be angry at her presumptuousness, or if I should burst out laughing.

"No," I finally say. I don't have the energy to cop an attitude.

As Dad and I walk back to the office, I listen to the voice mail Mom left during lunch. "Marcus," she says, her voice tinged with a maternal exasperation she has no right to, "I don't know why you're avoiding my calls, but I really need you to call me back. I'm worried about you. Your father called me and told me he's worried about you, and you know it would take a lot for him to do that—"

I hang up the phone before hearing the end of the message. "Jesus, Dad," I say, and stop walking. "I can't believe you."

"What?" he says. We're standing in the middle of the sidewalk on Market Street. An old Asian lady with a cart full of soda cans yells at us as she passes.

"Are you telling the whole Bay Area you're worried about me? Mom's been stalking me, and Monica tried to have a little heart-to-heart while you were in the bathroom. What the hell?"

He sighs. "I don't know what to do, Marcus. I'm trying everything."

"What to do about *what*? There's nothing to do. I'm fine."

"I may be pretty clueless as a father, but I can tell you're not fine. You stay holed up in your room whenever you're not at work. You don't go out. You don't see anyone."

"What I do with my free time is none of your business."

"I'm your father, Marcus. If you're miserable, it's my business. If you're . . . depressed. If you're in trouble somehow."

I start walking. "I'm not in trouble."

"You don't seem happy."

"What do you know about happy?"

"I know I wasted a lot of my life not thinking it was important. I know I don't want you to do that."

My stomach is churning with feelings I can't define. I don't know who I'm talking to. I don't understand what he's saying. We walk through the courthouse security and up the marble staircase to where all the offices are located.

"Talk to me," Dad says in the hallway outside the door to his office suite.

I open the door and walk inside, saying nothing. There's no way Dad will talk about this stuff in here, in front of his assistant. I know he has an important meeting in five minutes. I'm safe for now.

The next four hours drag. The adrenaline of my anger wears off quickly, and I'm left with an empty, heavy weight that makes it hard to lift my hands to type, to keep my eyes open. All I want to do is curl up in the pool of sunlight in the corner, like a cat. As soon as the clock strikes five, I can't get out of the building fast enough.

My phone shows another voice mail from Mom, which I don't listen to.

And then. A text from a number I don't recognize:

This is Evie. We need to talk. Can we meet at your house at 6?

I text back *yes* without thinking.

I could swim across the bay to meet her.

you.

I WANTED TO SAVE YOU. I WANTED TO BE THE SOLUTION TO all your pain. I thought if I could do that, then my life would be worth something. Then I'd have a reason to exist. Your love, your need, would create me. I would be born again, a hero.

But of course none of that is true. No one can ever really save anyone. No one can make you tell the truth or do the things that scare you. No one can force you to go inside yourself with your eyes open. No one can force you to come back out. No love is that strong.

I pulled you out of the water, yes. I kept you from drowning. But that kind of saving is easy. My job stopped there. You took your first breath, then it was up to you to do the rest. And up to me to find something else to do.

You could not save me, either. Did you know I had given you that job? Did I? Did you know you had the responsibility of becoming bigger than David, stronger than my mom, that you were supposed to be the sun and the moon and gravity and super-novas and dark matter—all of it? How did it feel to know you were expected to be everything?

It doesn't matter, if you knew or if you didn't. Either way, you'd be just as gone as you are now. And I'd be just as alone, just as haunted by the ghosts of my past. You have joined them; you have become a holy trinity—Mom, David, and Evie—the powers that rule me. I am your puppet. You three hold my strings, and it is up to me to cut them. It is up to me to save myself.

But I don't know if I can. I don't know if I'm that strong.

here.

THE DOORBELL RINGS A STRANGE, DEEP, FORMAL TUNE that echoes around the two-story living room, more like a funeral dirge than a greeting. I jump up from the hard surface of the couch, where I've been perched for the fifteen minutes since I've been home, waiting, vibrating with anticipation. I wouldn't call it excitement, but not quite dread either. It's a new kind of fear, one I can't define. I can't tell if it's good or bad.

When I open the door, Evie is surrounded by sunlight. Her hair is in a new pixie cut, more styled than the fluffy, haphazard chemo grow-out of before. She's wearing a light gray tank top and jeans with red Converse tennis shoes. Such a simple outfit, so clean and perfect. A thin silver ring loops around her left nostril.

"You got your nose pierced," I say.

"Yeah." She smiles. "Can I come in?"

"Oh," I say. "Yeah." I step aside.

"It was a birthday present, from my mom," she says as she

209

walks inside. "You should have seen her in the piercing studio." Evie laughs as she sits down on the couch. "She was trying so hard to act cool, but she was so awkward. It was hilarious."

I sit down across from her on an uncomfortable white leather armchair. "When was your birthday?" I say. How strange to not know that, to have never known that.

"Last week."

I can't bring my eyes to look at her face, so I stare at her knees, at her hands resting there, clasping and unclasping, naked of jewelry or nail polish.

"Why are you here?" I say, and it comes out sounding harsh, exactly as I'd intended it to.

She's quiet for a moment, then says quickly, "I met your mother."

"What?" My head snaps up. My eyes pierce hers.

"At an AA meeting." She looks more uncomfortable than I remember ever seeing her. Embarrassed, even. She looks down, squeezes her hands between her knees. "This is weird," she says. "I'm sorry."

"Come on. Tell me."

"She introduced herself after hearing me speak. I was talking about . . . you. And she recognized details of my story. And your name, too, I guess. So she approached me afterward."

"You talk about me at AA meetings?"

She cannot look me in the eyes. "People talk about everything at AA meetings. It's supposed to be anonymous, you know?"

"Except it wasn't."

"Well, no. Your mom probably broke all kinds of rules by talking to me, but she's so worried about you. She was desperate."

I can't help but laugh, but there's nothing funny about this. "Yeah," I say. "Desperate. We're all so fucking desperate."

"She really loves you. She's scared. She said you won't talk to her or your dad, so she asked me if I'd talk to you. She said she's afraid you might want to hurt yourself."

The ceiling is pressing down on us. The walls squeeze in. There are no words to speak, no air to breathe, no space to move in. The panic surges in my chest, and I am shaking with the need to run.

"I can't do this," I blurt out. "Not here. Not in this house." I stand up. "Can we go for a walk or something?"

"Um, sure," she says. "Okay." She grabs her bag and follows me out the door.

That's something I remember loving about her. She calls her purse a bag instead of a purse. She refused to be the kind of girl who carries a purse.

No. I have to push those kinds of thoughts out of my head now. All of her little endearing qualities. The little details I fell in love with.

Being outside gives my feelings room to grow. We walk a couple of blocks, and I notice Evie's limp is gone. For some reason, this makes me angry—her healing, her strength, all of it having happened without me, after all the energy and love I invested in her, in us. My anger feeds on the air, on the sun, becomes a monster, and consumes me.

"After all this time avoiding me, why come here now?" I say. "Why do you even care?"

"I care more than you could possibly know, Marcus." She sounds so patronizing. The way she says my name. The pitying tone of her voice.

"Yeah, you care so much you stopped talking to me."

"I had to. For a while. I already explained that to you." We stand at the corner waiting for the light to change. "I have to figure some things out," she says. "I need some time to clear my head."

"Yeah?" I start walking, even though the light is still red. A car honks as it barely misses me. "What about *my* head? Did you ever think about how it would affect me?"

"I'm sorry," she says, running after me to the other side of the street. She grabs my arm and makes me stop. "I thought you were okay. I thought you'd be okay. You were always the strong one."

I laugh, but there is no humor in it. "It's great you and my mom found each other," I say. "You have so much in common."

"What is that supposed to mean?"

"You both think because someone doesn't fall apart on a regular basis or go spewing their feelings all over the place, it means they can't get hurt. You think you can leave and they'll be fine, and you won't have to worry about breaking anyone's heart. Your conscience will be off the hook."

"No, that's not—"

"Just because my feelings aren't as messy as yours doesn't mean I don't have them."

"Marcus, I—"

"Yours were so big and loud, there wasn't any room for mine."

The silence burns as I walk away, and for the first time ever, *she* runs after *me*. So I let her chase me. I want her to know what it feels like to be shut out.

But eventually, I slow down. The truth is, as much as I want to hurt her, I still want her next to me.

"You've changed," she says.

"Being betrayed will do that to a person."

She flinches, takes a deep breath. My body still responds to hers, even after these weeks apart. "I've been preparing what I wanted to say to you for a long time," she says. "But I kept chickening out when I tried to call you. Then your mom approached me, and I figured it was a sign that it was time to talk."

Without thinking, I have led us to the cemetery where we went on our first date. Where we first made love. I fight the urge to turn around. I walk through the iron gates to the big fountain near the entrance. The sound of the water silences everything around us. I sit on a stone bench facing it.

"So talk," I say.

After a pause, she says, "You want someone you think is me."

I don't say anything. The sentence hangs in the air, all alone, without context.

"I'm not her. I'm not the girl you loved. The one you think you want. That girl who acted invincible."

"What are you talking about?" The water in the fountain falls in slow motion.

"That girl was made out of drugs and alcohol and lies. She wasn't me."

"You can't tell me you weren't in there. You can't tell me that wasn't you at all."

"But it wasn't all of me."

"So show me all of you!" Evie flinches. My hands are shaking and my body throbs with electricity. People look. Dogs sniff the air, smelling something sinister. They think I am the kind of guy who yells at his girlfriend in public. Maybe I am. Maybe I'm more like my father than I've ever wanted to admit.

"I don't know how," she says quietly. "I don't know who that is."

I am sick of this bullshit. I'm sick of dancing around the truth.

"Do you still love me?" I say.

"Marcus, don't."

"Answer the question."

"You're changing the subject. It's irrelevant."

"Love's irrelevant?" I hear my father's voice. I hear myself debating like him, asking questions that cannot be answered.

"You're not listening."

"Why won't you answer the question?"

She's shutting down. Her eyes lose focus and her hands fidget. She's putting up her wall. She's leaving me.

"Answer the question, Evie. Do you love me?"

She shakes her head and says nothing. Her shoulders curl as she closes in on herself.

"Does that mean no? You don't love me?"

She says no so quietly I might not have heard her if I wasn't staring at her quivering lips.

"No, what?"

"Yes," she whispers.

"What?" I say. "I can't hear you."

"Yes!" she yells. "Dammit, Marcus. Yes, of course I still fucking love you."

Her body shakes in the silence. I want to take back everything, all my pushing, my bullying. But I can't. Neither of us can ever take back anything we've done to each other.

"That's not the problem," Evie says. "That's never been the problem. I just . . . how can I trust my love for you when I don't know who I am? How can that love possibly make any sense?"

"Maybe love's not supposed to make sense."

She shakes her head slowly. "I lost myself somewhere," she says quietly. "I used to think I knew exactly who I was. I never questioned it. I didn't have to. There was this version of me that existed before the cancer, some girl I don't even recognize."

"The cheerleader girl."

"Yeah," she says with a self-hating smirk. "You would have hated her. The cheerleader with the long blond hair and the perfectly nice football boyfriend."

"I wouldn't have hated her."

"I do."

"Why?"

She's quiet for a moment as she stares at the fountain. "I hate her because I'm jealous. Her life was so simple. It was so easy being her."

"But she isn't you."

"Not anymore. Even if I wanted to be her again, I couldn't. Getting sick changed everything, and I can't ever go back. I became a different version of me, the dying version."

"But you're not dying anymore."

"No, but I accepted that was the last me there was going to be." She's growing agitated. Her voice is shaky, angry. She's talking fast. "But I didn't die. So I had to become yet another version of myself. Even though I didn't want to. Even though I was done. So I had to get high to deal with it, just to make it not hurt. And I lied to everyone. I lied to you." She's crying now. She leans over her knees, her face in her hands. "That's the girl you knew. That's who you fell in love with. But she doesn't exist anymore either." I can see the bones of her spine through smooth skin as her body quakes. Fragile, worn, breaking. I fight the urge to touch her. I don't know if I have that right anymore.

"I'm not her, Marcus," Evie cries. "I'm not that wild girl who wants to party. I'm not that girl who doesn't give a shit about anything."

"I never thought you were," I say, wanting so much to hold her, to make her understand. The girl she's talking about is not who I loved. That's who I wanted to save her from.

Evie looks at me and blinks, like my response was not the one she expected. "You gave a shit about something," I say. "You gave a shit about me. That was real. I felt it."

She sniffles and looks at me, into my eyes. "You were the only thing I cared about," she says, letting me in, and my heart leaps into hers.

"Yes." I take her hand and hold it against my heart. For a moment, it feels perfect. For a moment, it feels like the world is starting again. But then she pulls her hand away. Her eyes turn back into ice.

"No," she says, shaking her head. "Marcus, don't you see? That's not the way it's supposed to be. You can't be the only thing. You can't be the thing that defines me."

"I never asked to be. It doesn't have to be like that."

"But I don't know how to do anything else."

Neither of us know what to say after that. We sit there for a while, exhausted, surrounded by the dense cloud of our words. Nothing is settled. Nothing is resolved. The fountain continues its circular flow. Coins glisten on the tile bottom, a collection of strangers' wishes and dreams. I reach into my pocket and pull out a quarter. I cannot hear its splash as I add my dream to the anonymous others.

"So now what?" I finally say.

"I don't know."

"So am I allowed to call you now that I have your new number?" I try to make it sound funny, but it falls flat. It belly flops in the fountain. It drowns.

Evie is quiet for a long time, and the beginning of hope flutters in my chest, my heart a hummingbird. My hand begins to move from its place on the concrete bench, a slight stirring, on the way to find hers where it rests on her knees.

"No," she says finally. Firmly.

My hand stops in midair, sinks back to the hard flatness of the bench. My coin is lost among the other wasted money in the fountain.

She shakes her head with her eyes closed. "I'm not ready. Not yet." Then her eyes open and tear me apart. "Maybe not ever."

Evie's eyes bore into me, but I will not look at her. I can't. "I need you to let me go, Marcus," she says, and my head is filled with static, loud and grating.

"Fine," I say, my voice as cruel as I've ever heard it. "Go."

She doesn't move.

"Go!"

She stands up. She starts walking. She leaves too easily.

Stop! I want to say. *Come back!*

I wait for her to turn around, to look back, to say something, to make things right, to apologize, explain, anything. But she says nothing. She keeps walking away, holding her bag tight against her body. I sit on the hard bench, my feet heavy on the ground, fighting the rising fire in my chest, the tears in my eyes, waiting for a look that never comes. Just the sound of the fountain, so loud I can't hear Evie's footsteps as she leaves me, again.

you.

THE DEAD SEAGULL ON THE BEACH WAS A SIGN. I SHOULD have known something bad was going to happen. The rocks crunched beneath my feet as I jogged to keep up with you. As always, I chased you. You had already drunk half the bottle of vodka in the car, but somehow you were still so fast.

You held court on a stage of driftwood. Your hands waved in the air as you recounted the story that led you to this place. It was impossible to know where to find the truth between your words, which parts were facts and which parts were the stories you attached to your feelings. Emotions have a way of warping the truth, of twisting it around until it is all just a story you tell yourself over and over to keep yourself crazy.

The scent of decay and dirty seawater was thick as you told me about your life falling apart, about failing school, about your best friend hating you, about your mom and dad disappointed beyond repair. You listed all the ways life was failing you, all the ways you were abandoned, but you said nothing about your own lies, about the drugs you couldn't stop doing, about the promises you couldn't keep. You said nothing about your own responsibility.

I could have kept going along with it. I could have kept quiet about the self-destruction that was becoming more apparent every day, every hour that I loved you. But I was tired, Evie. I was so tired of watching you hurt, so tired of listening to you blame the world for your pain. So I had to say something. I had to finally speak.

I wanted your pain to stop, too. Can't you see that's all I ever wanted for you? I knew what you were doing wasn't working. What David did hadn't worked. My mom's drinking hadn't worked. So I cried for all of you. I sat there looking out at the water, at the postcard view of San Francisco, and I suddenly knew there was a very good chance that I was going to lose you, too.

here.

I WAKE UP KNOWING SOMETHING HAS TO CHANGE. I FEEL it in my bones. Before I even open my eyes, the thought burns through the fog in my head, in blinking neon lights: this is the day the bullshit ends.

My phone dings with a text message.

Evie told me about your meeting yesterday, says the text from Mom. *Can we get together to talk? I want to support you during this difficult time. Love you.*

It is the Hallmark card of text messages. It is empty words.

Not even awake ten minutes, and I'm already supremely grumpy as I walk downstairs to get some coffee.

I'm used to the kitchen being empty and silent when I enter it in the morning. I have a routine. I make two cups of coffee in the Keurig and pour them into my giant mug. I make a piece of toast and retreat back to my lair. But this morning is all wrong. I hear laughter before I even get there. I smell bacon.

Dad is sitting at the kitchen table while Monica cooks. "Morning!" he says, way too enthusiastically.

"Want some bacon?" Monica chimes in. She's wearing a pair of Dad's pajama pants and an old T-shirt.

"I'm vegetarian," I say flatly, the only excuse I can think of that could possibly justify saying no to bacon.

"I just made a fresh pot of coffee," she says. I can't remember the last time we used the coffeepot. That would imply sharing. That would imply some kind of coordinated effort. We usually make our own individual cups in the Keurig.

"Thanks," I say, and grab a mug to fill as quickly as possible so I can get out of here.

"Marcus," Dad says, "sit down for a minute, will you?"

"What's up?" I eye him skeptically.

"I want to talk to you about something."

I look at Monica, who's smiling as she pats the grease off the hot bacon. Whatever my dad's about to talk to me about, she's in on it too.

I sit and take a sip of my coffee. The proportions are all wrong. As if my day wasn't sucking enough already. "This coffee's too weak," I say.

"Oh, sorry," Monica apologizes. "I can make a new pot if you want." Dad glares at me.

"No, it's okay," I say. I'll sneak the real stuff when no one's looking. I don't want Monica doing me any favors.

"Marcus," Dad says seriously. He has his judge face on. "How are you feeling today?"

I'm caught off guard. "Fine," I say.

"I want to talk to you about something," he says for the second time. He looks down at his hands, and I see a trace of sadness on his face before he hides it, and my heart burns hot in my chest for a painful second before it goes numb.

"Just say it, Dad."

My father, who is afraid of nothing, looks scared.

"I miss him, too," he finally says. Monica sits next to him and puts her arm around him. "I miss David," he says quietly, almost a whisper.

Time stops and I am stuck somewhere unfamiliar, a different world, a different dimension. This is the first time I've heard David's name come out of Dad's mouth since the surreal few weeks after his death; the few times he mentioned him, it was always "your brother," as if he didn't have a claim to him. But his name was only business then, a problem to be dealt with, a funeral to plan. His name was just a word. But now it is new and tragic in my father's mouth, with a year's worth of hidden pain holding on to it, and I cannot take it. I cannot listen. I am suffocating under its weight.

"I have to go," I say, standing up.

"Marcus, wait," Dad says. "We need to talk about it. About him. We can't keep pretending nothing happened."

"But that's what we're good at, Dad. That's the only thing we know how to do."

I storm out of the kitchen without my coffee. I hear the screeching of Dad's chair as he gets up. I hear Monica's gentle voice say,

"Let him go. He'll be ready to talk in his own time." When did she become such an expert on our family? When did she get the right to tell my dad what to do?

I run up the stairs and down the hall of the side of the house Dad never enters, open the door that no one's touched in months. Inside the room is very little I recognize. Just storage, just garbage. Random pieces of furniture that have no place in the house. Boxes of stuff no one's used in years. The only thing left of David's is the old dresser that belonged to my great-grandfather, which my uncle made Dad promise not to throw away. The walls were repainted soon after David's death, all of his stuff bagged up and donated to Goodwill. I had barely saved his plants from being thrown away like everything else Dad got rid of without even asking me.

It was three months ago that I came in here and found an old pack of David's cigarettes in the dresser, three months since I stole his ashes from the mantel and poured them in the bay, three months since I discovered Evie in the dark of the tunnel. So much has happened in the short time since then, it'd be funny if it wasn't so fucking sad.

I sit in the middle of the floor, still in my pajama pants and faded Nirvana T-shirt. I look at the dresser, trying to channel him, trying to feel something, anything of David. I close my eyes and try to picture him, try to see his face lit by the sun, try to see his smile. But all I see is a distorted, broken version of him, his features misplaced like a Picasso painting. I squint and force them back to where they belong, but his face becomes a mess of black and brown and gray. It swirls into itself until all I see is a black hole where his face should be.

I don't remember what my brother looks like.

I am sitting in this soulless room trying to conjure a ghost. He's gone. He's been gone for a long time. But I keep carrying him around with me like a curse.

I jump up. I run to my room. Even without my morning caffeine, I am suddenly buzzing with energy. But it is not the kind of energy that feels good, not the alert high of caffeine, not the rumbling excitement of being at a punk show, not the hot thrill of sex. It is something dark. Destructive. Like a lightning strike. Like electrocution.

The summer morning light shines in sharp lines through the blinds, cutting my bedroom into thin pieces. I want to grab the beams and throw them. I want to whack them against the wall and hear them shatter. David's plants sit in pots scattered throughout my room, droopy with fatigue from my desperate attempts to keep them alive. They knew when to give up. They knew when to let go even if I didn't.

I pull the string of my window shades and sunlight pours into my room, an avalanche, a tidal wave of light, everything exposed. There are no hiding places. I push open my window and breathe in the last evaporating particles of dew, before the brief freshness of the morning is lost and replaced by the grime of the city.

I grab the nearest plant and throw.

The pot smashes on the brick patio beneath my window. Dirt and shards of pottery go flying. I throw and throw and throw. Ivy, succulents, ferns, spider plants, a bamboo palm, a peace lily.

When I lift a five-foot-tall ficus in a thick clay pot, I feel a familiar twinge in my shoulder, but it doesn't even slow me down.

There's a tornado inside me and it's spinning out of control. It's been gaining momentum for months, for years, but only in the past weeks has it touched ground and made its destruction known. I thought it was about Evie. I thought it was about David, or Mom, or Dad. But the storm rages on regardless of what they do, regardless of their cruelty or kindness or indifference. They don't touch it. They are not strong enough to make the weather.

I am the only constant in this storm. I am the only one who can stop it.

The plants are all gone. I am the only visible living thing left in my room.

I go to the box in the back of my closet where I kept my treasures as a young boy, then my drugs, then my razor blades. It is empty now except for one thing.

I take out the smaller black wooden box inside. I open it to make sure everything is there, to make sure the gun has not been stolen by some rival ghost, to make sure it still belongs to the proper thief.

I pull on a pair of jeans crumpled on my floor. I throw the box in my backpack. I run out of the house without tying my shoes. The tornado follows.

here.

I am driving. The route is burned into my memory. Evie is the last person who sat in the passenger's seat.

there.

The house is louder after Mom leaves than it was when she was in it. Workers in heavy boots stomp in and out, a human conveyor belt made out of strangers, carrying furniture, art, bags and boxes of Mom's things she didn't take with her. Out goes the homey stuff I grew up with; in comes the furniture that is meant to be looked at but not touched, sharp and shiny and starkly beautiful. My father's choices.

you.

You tasted death, then came back from it. How many people can claim that kind of magic? How many people can say they conquered cancer?

You heard death calling you, luring you back to it with candy. You tasted it, devoured it, then spit it back out just in time.

But now what? What do you hear? Can you hear anything besides your own voice?

You never asked to be a miracle.

here.

The water crashes below me. Just a rail between me and the sea. A gun in my backpack, already claimed by death.

there.

Blood. So much blood.

you.

Not blood. Water.

here.

The air is so hot. The metal is so cold.

you.

Hospitals, coffee shops, beaches, cemeteries. Hills, grass, space, and stars. The places you made your home. Basements, tunnels. My life, my heart.

there.

David's initials, the skeleton of his name, carved into my body. The pain keeps the tears from coming. I choose blood instead of tears.

here.

A scar, one year old. No longer the pink of new skin. No longer tender to the touch. Just smooth raised lines the color of myself, but bleached.

DL, and the date this gun last fired. These self-inflicted rips in my flesh are all that's left of my brother.

you.

Cold. Wet. Barely breathing. Barely holding on.

there.

Silence.

you.

Breath.

there.

Nothing.

you.

The light in the darkness.

here.

I am all I have left.

now.

I AM STANDING ON THE NEW BAY BRIDGE, LOOKING AT THE concrete skeleton of the old bridge. Cormorants and other birds have reclaimed it as their home. They swarm close, like bees around their hive.

The wind screams in my ears. Cars speed by on the freeway, with only a thin fence separating me from several lanes of traffic. Waves crash far below and the birds screech their displeasure at the cold spray. But up here, the wind is hot and the sun beats down on my skin. It is so loud, no one would hear me if I screamed. I am an unnamed stranger among so many unnamed strangers. If I disappeared, I would not be missed.

I cannot see our beach from here. It is on the other side of the bridge, where there's no place for pedestrians, just cars, just traffic.

Families on bicycles coast by me. Couples walk, hand in hand. Joggers run. They are never going to make it to San Francisco this way. The pedestrian lane stops unceremoniously in the middle of nowhere, in the middle of air, before it even reaches Yerba Buena Island. All we can do is look at the place we cannot go, then turn around and go back where we came from.

It's so strange that Evie and I never came up here, considering all the time we spent in places so close. But we preferred to go where others didn't. Dark places. Hidden. Places where we would not be seen. What were we so scared of? What were we trying to hide?

God, I am so sick of hiding.

Nobody cares about the Bay Bridge. It's not the Golden Gate, not a tourist destination, not the number one place in the world to commit suicide. Is it as deadly? Is it high enough to kill me if I jump? Is the water below as rough and full of sharks? Would my body be broken by the fall? Would it wash up on my beach, on Evie's and David's and Mom's beach, in the same place where I found Evie, almost dead, in the same place where I freed David's ashes? All three of us, returned to the water. Together.

Here's a bench to look out at the view. Here's a pole with an emergency phone. Here I am, climbing onto the railing. It's too easy. It's like they want people to die. They want word to spread about how easy it is to climb the fence here; it's not just the Golden Gate that's great for jumping.

It's a beautiful day on the bay. It was a beautiful day when I found David in his apartment with his head blown off. It was a beautiful day when I found Evie, facedown in this water. The day Mom left. The days I cut myself, when I drew my own blood to make the pain stop, those were beautiful days, too. The sun is always shining in Oakland, as if people aren't dying all over the place, as if people's lives aren't falling apart.

No one even sees me standing up here. They are too busy looking at the city in the distance. They are too distracted by beauty to see the ugliness right here in front of them.

But I can't ignore the ugliness. No matter how hard I shut my eyes, I see horror and heartbreak and the pain of everyone I love. It seeps into me and becomes my pain, their blood my blood, and I can't tell where I stop and they begin. Love pulls me in every direction; it gets distorted into poison and tears me apart.

I will never be able to save them. It is not in my power to make them stay. They make that choice and there is nothing I can do about it.

This ends now.

I hold on tight to the pole as I grab my backpack from my back, as I pull the zipper open. A gust of wind blows me off balance and makes my heart jump, and I hold on even tighter as I try to keep the world from spinning. I take out Dad's black box and pull out the gun.

Guns are designed to end things. It is their only job.

The silver metal glistens in the sun. I study every inch of it, turn it over in my hands, again searching for some sign that the small, hard thing is responsible for ending my brother. Strange how he was the one who always hated it, who never wanted to be anywhere near it when we were kids. Strange how it was the last thing that kept him company, probably the last thing he ever saw.

The gun is just a thing, a piece of molded metal. But I look at it and see the people I love; I feel the weight of our stories as I hold it in my hand. I spin the cylinder and it sounds like our voices. I hear Mom crying. I hear Dad yelling. I hear David, I hear Evie, begging God to make their pain go away. All this time, I thought they were talking to me. I thought God's job was mine.

So many choices. So many ways to live and die. So many ways to give power and to take it. So many ways to begin and end. So many ways to hold on and let go.

So many ways to say good-bye. So many ways for lives to end.

I thought I was saying good-bye to David when I threw his ashes into the sea. But it's not that simple. This good-bye will last forever. This good-bye will haunt me until the day I die. Only then will I stop missing him.

But that day is not today.

So many lives. So many ways to start over.

I throw the gun over the edge. I watch it fly through the air, catching flashes of sunlight on its way down. I see the small splash but cannot hear it over the cacophony of everything else in the world. It is in darkness now, where it belongs. Sinking, soundless. Turned into just another rock at the bottom of the sea.

Good-bye, David. Good-bye, mother and father of my childhood. Good-bye, Evie of the tunnel, Evie of the beach, Evie of hiding and secrets and shame. I say good-bye and I will keep saying good-bye. I am letting you go. I free you. I free us all.

now.

IT IS EARLY EVENING WHEN I GET HOME, MY BACKPACK empty, the gun and box and bullets deep in the bay. The house smells like food again, as if Dad and Monica have been cooking all day.

I open the door to the kitchen and am shocked to find Mom in there with them. I stand motionless for several moments, trying to understand what I am seeing: Dad, at the counter, chopping vegetables; Mom and Monica, side by side at the stove, stirring things in pots.

What is going on?

Dad looks up from his lettuce. "Marcus!" he says, as if genuinely happy to see me. I've never seen him this happy to be chopping vegetables.

"Hey" is the only thing I can think to say to the weird scene in front of me. No one seems worried or anxious. They must not have noticed the dirt and plants and broken pots piled beneath my bedroom window. They know nothing of where I've been, what I might have done.

"You're just in time for dinner," Mom says, then throws her arms around me. "Oh, it's so good to see you."

"What are you doing here?" I say, not rudely. Just confused. This is not the mother I said good-bye to on the bridge. This is not the mother I let go. She is someone new. She is trying to be someone new.

"Your dad called and invited me over for dinner. I knew it had to be Monica's idea, but I came anyway." She and Monica wink at each other. "Bill could never come up with something like that on his own."

"Who's hungry?" Monica calls cheerfully from the stove. "I can't eat this whole batch of spaghetti carbonara on my own."

"I'm starving," Mom says.

"Bill, how's that salad coming?" Monica says.

"Uh," Dad says, looking over at his station of mangled vegetables. "I think I may need some help."

Mom and Monica laugh and share a knowing look. I feel like I've walked on to the set of a sitcom about an alternative Bay Area family.

"Wait a minute," I say. "Stop." The three of them look at me—Dad, Mom, and apparently her new bestie, Monica. "Am I the only one here who thinks this is really fucking weird?"

They all look at each other, then burst into laughter. "It is what it is," Mom says as she takes over Dad's place at the counter to finish the salad. "I think we're all figuring this out as we go along."

As we all sit down to eat, I feel strangely optimistic. Maybe I can get used to this new weird family. Slowly. In small doses. At least the food is way better than the garbage Dad and I have been living on for the last two years.

I will tell him about the gun, but not now. Right now, I'm going to enjoy this dinner. There's been enough drama. But I have a feeling Dad won't be too upset. I don't think he'll mind the gun being lost forever.

"I'd like to make a toast," Dad says. He and Monica raise their wineglasses. Mom and I raise glasses of lemonade Monica made from scratch.

"Since we're all here together, I want us to take a moment to remember David," Dad says. My heart catches in my throat. My blood stops. "He was our beloved son and brother, and we miss him." Dad chokes on the last words.

"To David," Mom says. She is smiling, beautiful. "My baby."

And I am crying. I am shaking with deep, heavy sobs that come from somewhere across time and space, from deep inside the earth where they have been stored for all these years, waiting to be released. But this is not all of them. This purging will not be the end of pain. There will always be more. There will be new things to hurt about and old things to remember, but maybe I won't have to store them for so long, maybe I won't have to wrap them so tight and hide them away inside myself. I won't have to let them fester and grow and become even more toxic. I can release the pain. I can let it go by feeling it.

Dad reaches across the table and puts his hand on mine. Mom

wraps her arm around my shoulders and pulls me into her. "Oh, honey," she says. "Oh, my poor, poor baby." Both of us, her babies. One gone, but one very much still here.

I let her hold me until the wave subsides. I don't have a name for it—sadness, pain, mourning—it is all those things and more. But also gratitude. Also love. The feelings are huge, but there is room for all of them. There is a place where they are safe.

I look up at these three faces, two of which I've been looking at my whole life, but all of which I'm only now really starting to know.

I raise my glass. "To David," I say.

"And to us," Dad adds. "To family."

"Here, here," Monica says.

We say "cheers." We start eating, all of our faces still wet with tears. It is the best meal I've had in a long time.

now.

MOM SAYS IT'S TRAGIC THAT THE BAY AREA DOESN'T HAVE seasons. She says it screws with our circadian rhythms or something. But I've never known any different, so it feels like fall to me, even if it is seventy degrees during the day. There are a few trees here and there with leaves changing color. Night has been coming a little sooner each day.

I have a big project due in my Political Science class before Thanksgiving break and I've had to work with a partner, which is something I would have usually detested, but it hasn't actually been that bad. James is pretty cool. I've gotten to know him since I stopped sitting at the lunch table with the stoners and started sitting with him and a handful of guys who are all pretty different in mostly interesting ways. They're not "cool," but they're not losers. They're the kinds of guys who fly under the radar in high school because their focus is elsewhere, on the future, on becoming bigger versions of themselves.

I'm riding in James's car. We've been mostly working at his house in the Berkeley Hills, but today he wanted a change of scenery. He's probably sick of his mom checking on our progress every half hour.

"Where should we go?" he says. "Somewhere on Piedmont? College?"

"What about Telegraph?"

"Berkeley or Oakland?"

"Oakland, obviously."

I don't know what I'm thinking. It's like there's a beacon inside my head, blinking, beeping, telling me my destination, opening my mouth and speaking the directions to James. Another part of my brain says *Are you crazy?* but I can barely hear it.

James parks in front of the yoga studio and we get out of the car. A tilting man with bloodshot eyes stumbles in front of a perky, ponytailed woman pushing a stroller and talking on her cell phone. What a strange place this is, all these worlds bumping into each other and barely even noticing.

As James opens the door to the café, I stop dead in my tracks.

"Dude, are you coming?" James says.

It's then that I know. I just know. I feel it in my bones. Evie's here.

"Yeah," I say. "I'm coming."

There is no feeling of surprise when I see her standing at the counter with Cole. Just a warmth that starts in my feet and moves up into the center of me. But it is heavy and I can't move. I stand there, staring at her, watching her easy laugh, feeling both like I know her, all of her, but we've barely met. It's been months since we've seen each other, months of my trying to let her go. I'm a different person now. She's different. Everything's different.

James approaches the counter and orders his drink from Cole, who hasn't noticed me yet. I count quietly to myself, *one, two, three*, and then Evie's eyes meet mine like I knew they would, as if we are driven by the same timing. The dopey grin spreads across my face. Her smile is warm, pure, radiating.

I don't know how long we stare at each other. I don't know how long James has been elbowing me in the side, saying, "Dude. Dude. *Dude*."

"Oh," I say. "Hey, James."

"Are you going to order something or just stand there?"

"James," I say, "I'd like you to meet my old friend Evie."

"Hi, Evie," he says suspiciously.

"Nice to meet you, James." Her smile is soft. Peaceful.

"Yeah, um," James says, "I'm going to sit down now."

"Marcus," Evie says, "this is my friend Cole."

Cole smiles warmly. "Hi, Marcus."

"Hey," I say. "We already met," I tell Evie.

"Oh yeah." She laughs. "I forgot you came here snooping on me a while back." She says this playfully, with no trace of anger.

"It's been a while," I say.

"Yes," she says. "It has." She smiles, and I wonder if she's thinking the same thing I am, that maybe it has been a perfect amount of time that has passed, that maybe now is a perfect time for it to be over.

"It's good to see you," I say.

"Yes," she says. "It is."

Or maybe not. What if we're still bad for each other? What if we're still poison? She said before that I inspired her recklessness. I know now that I turned her into an extension of David, that I let her self-destruction define our love. That can't be what we are to each other. Not anymore. Not ever again.

So what if we start over from the beginning? What if we start by telling each other everything?

We stand there for a long time, staring at each other. There's so much to say, we are only capable of silence.

"Hey," Cole says, and it's only then, when the coffee shop suddenly explodes with movement and noise, that I realize time had paused in those short moments—everyone had stopped moving, the espresso machine stopped steaming, the coffee grinder stopped grinding, and the only thing that existed was the space between me and Evie, the energy passing between us, the question we were asking each other with our eyes: *Should we try this again?*

"Evie and I were talking about going to a movie later," Cole says, and his voice calms me. I hardly know him, but something tells me I want to.

We both look at him. I notice a quick glance between him and Evie, a playful glint in Cole's eyes.

"Want to join us, Marcus?" he says.

I look at Evie, searching her face for apprehension, for a sign that this is not what she wants. I feel a moment of panic. Is this what I want? But it is only a moment, small and fleeting. "Really?" I say.

"Yeah," she says. "The more the merrier."

What could our relationship look like when neither of us need saving?

My heart is beating so fast I think it might fly out of here. I look at Cole, who seems amused by the whole awkward situation. "Will that be weird for you?" I ask him. I think I am sweating.

He throws his head back in a big laugh. "I think I'm probably going be the most comfortable of all of us."

us.

YOU ARE SITTING IN THE PASSENGER SEAT, YOUR WINDOW half rolled down, your short hair fluttering in the wind like wildflowers. In the forty minutes or so since we got off the freeway, we've driven through forest, farmland, and a handful of small towns, the Russian River faithfully on our left, dotted by the occasional kayak or canoe.

"I can smell the sea," you say, closing your eyes and inhaling deep.

I can, too. One small hill stands in the way of perfect blue sky and our destination. We are only two hours away from the city, but we are in a different world, one without billboards and crowds and traffic and noise. Cows munch grass in front of a picturesque old farmhouse. We crest the hill and the Pacific Ocean swallows the earth in front of us. I forget that I'm driving, and we fly the rest of the way to the edge of the continent.

The sand takes our toes. The sun warms our bones. We are

on the edge of the world, on earth that was just born. We are new people, falling in love for the first time. Again and again and again.

"I love this emergency nap blanket," you say. You are in my arms. We are facing the sea. Waves hypnotize us with their rhythm.

I think about the times we have spent on this blanket, all those moments we used it to make ourselves an island, which we tucked away on hidden beaches, on tops of hills, behind bushes and driftwood and gravestones. We are not hiding now, but there is a solitude, still the sense of a world that is only ours. But it is not a dangerous world. It is made out of clean sand and ocean breeze and a safe distance from the waves and riptides.

You sigh. "I wonder how long it's going to stay wild like this, before humans fuck it up."

You push yourself into me. We make a more perfect spoon. "Let's not worry about that right now," I say.

"Okay." But after a minute, you say, "Why did God even bother making humans? We must be such huge disappointments."

"Maybe not."

"But we ruin everything we touch."

"Not everything. We make music and art and write books. We love each other."

"When did you get so optimistic?"

I squeeze you tighter. "You make me feel optimistic."

A long-beaked bird pecks at the sand in front of us. A wave crashes inches from his little bird feet, but he doesn't even seem to notice. He is at peace with his rough world.

"My brother had this theory that the way a person, or even an entire culture, thinks about God is the way they think about their fathers," I say. "Like we all want God to be this kind, nurturing dude full of forgiveness and unconditional love, but what most people actually believe is that God's this hateful, mean guy who we'll never please no matter what we do. Either that or he's totally absent or nonexistent."

"That's depressing."

"David could be a depressing guy," I say. "But he could also be really funny. No one's ever made me laugh like him."

"I wish I could have met him."

"Yeah," I say. "Me, too."

After a moment, you say, "But maybe it doesn't have to be depressing—David's theory. Because relationships can change, right? If people can change, then maybe so can God."

You turn around and face me. Your eyes are everything. I wrap you in my arms and bury myself in your neck. I breathe in your sweetness with the salt.

"Do you think there's more?" you say. "More than us? More than this?"

Of course there's more. There is a whole ocean once you get out of the bay.

Acknowledgments

Thank you to Ben Rosenthal for your insight and guidance on this book, and for taking such good care of me from the very start.

Thank you to everyone at Katherine Tegen and HarperCollins who worked on *Unforgivable* and *Invincible*. Thank you especially to artist Julie McLaughlin and jacket designer Heather Daugherty for creating such powerful, beautiful covers.

Huge thanks, as always, to my agent and fiercest cheerleader, Amy Tipton.

Odd's Café in Asheville, North Carolina, for giving me such a cozy place to write when my home office gets too lonely.

Malaprop's Bookstore, for your loving and enthusiastic support of the Asheville YA author community.

Everytown for Gun Safety (www.everytown.org) for providing the stats about guns and for the great work you do fighting for gun control in America.

My husband, Brian, for being my biggest fan and best beta reader. I love your guts.

My daughter, Elouise, for inspiring me to start believing in happy endings.

And finally, a huge thank-you and profound gratitude to Anica Rissi, whose imagination gave birth to Evie and Marcus, and who trusted me to adopt them and raise them as my own. So many years ago, I trusted you with my first book baby, *Beautiful*, and since then you have been a constant in my writing life. Thank you for believing in me at the beginning when I needed it so much. I am a better writer because of you. I will miss you as you embark on new adventures, but I believe in you, too.

FOLLOW THE INCREDIBLE STORY OF

EVIE and MARCUS

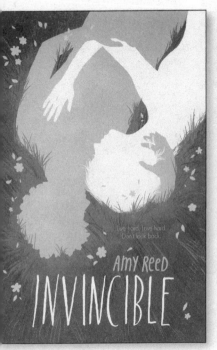

in this intense, romantic duology by
AMY REED